TO THE G

Peter Levi, classical scholar, ~~archaeologist~~ and poet, was born in Ruislip in 1931. He has taught Greek, Latin and archaeology. He has been a priest, a prison chaplain, and archaeological correspondent for *The Times*, a schoolmaster, a don and a travel writer. His works include *The Hill of Kronos*, *The Flutes of Autumn* and *Grave Witness*. He is a fellow of St Catherine's College Oxford and professor of poetry at Oxford University.

ARENA
NOVELLA

TO THE GOAT

Peter Levi

ARENA
NOVELLA

For Deidre

You lovers, for whose sake the lesser Sun
At this time to the Goat is run
To fetch new lust, and give it you,
Enjoy your summer all;

John Donne's *Nocturnal Upon St Lucy's Day*

An Arena Book
Published by Arrow Books Limited
62–65 Chandos Place, London WC2N 4NW

An imprint of Century Hutchinson Limited

London Melbourne Sydney Auckland
Johannesburg and agencies throughout
the world

First published in Great Britain in 1988 by
Century Hutchinson Limited
in the Hutchinson Novella series

Arena edition 1989

Typeset in Monophoto Photina by
Vision Typesetting, Manchester

Printed in Great Britain by
The Guernsey Press Co. Ltd,
Guernsey C. I.

ISBN 0 09 9633809

PART ONE

England was dark green with straw-coloured patches, and the vicars were smiling like crocodiles. The freezing wind and long uncertainty of spring were quite forgotten, now nettles darkened under hedges, apples were ripening, schools and colleges had shut their doors. Buck was in search of work.

He stepped down from a country bus near the gates of a large country house. It had woods and a lake, and a herd of black and white goats fenced in with electric wire. Its avenue was long and sinuous, but the day was hot and he enjoyed the adventure and the walk. He was a poet feeling his oats. He had a degree, not a good one but better than he deserved, and he had a book out from a good publisher. They had paid him a hundred pounds in advance. Now he was going to live in the country by tutoring, if only he survived the interview; he had the idea of working on the sex life of the royal family, 1882–1982. That ought to make more than a hundred pounds. And the little boy could live *à l'ombre d'un jeune poète en fleur*, and pass his beastly Common Entrance. Maths was going to be difficult, because Buck had forgotten how to do long division, but Latin was his washpot and over English he had flung his shoe.

Poets at that age are all much the same, nervous and bony, and very conscious of their individuality. The critics had been kind to Buck, kinder indeed than they ever would be again until his hair was white. Even the feminist critics liked him, because they could see that he liked them. He was one of the new wave of readable poets, an upmarket version of Gavin Ewart with touches of what you might call bodyline yuppy. You would never guess all that from seeing him walk up the drive, with his dark knitted tie and his white shirt and his coat over one shoulder.

The house was not in the first rank or the second rank of houses. It was like a seaside house only bigger, squatter, more comfortable-looking. Sir James Haddalot had bought a Victorian castle for its park, and blown up the castle. This had been a steward's house, hence the sinuous avenue that led to it. Sir James liked the idea of hiring a poet for the summer.

'Welcome aboard. Ha!'

'Thank you, sir.'

'So you're the poet?'

'Well – er – yes.'

'Ha! Any experience?'

'Er – not really. This is my first job.'

'Mmm. Play cricket?'

'Not too well.'

'Ha! But you play? Hamsyn likes cricket. About all he does like.'

'Ah, I see.'

'Make him work, Ha? Two hours a day, five days a week. And be company for him. Make yourself useful at weekends, when we have people. That suit you, Ha.'

The last 'Ha' was not quite interrogative, it was more of a signature on a contract. There appeared to be no question of Buck not getting the job, that possibility seemed to occur to neither of them.

'When do I meet him?'

'Meet him? Mmm. At tea. We have that through the door there, between those two modern pictures. You can teach him in this room, Ha. In the morning.'

'Fine. The pictures are nice. Who are they by?'

'That one's Braque and that one's Picasso. You interested in pictures?'

'Yes.'

'For God's sake never touch one in this house, even if it's hanging crooked. Ha! An alarm goes off in the police station. Oh and never come downstairs before they call you. Ha! Burglar alarms have to be switched off.'

It was Buck's first lesson in how the rich live. He had never been inside a really rich man's house before. It was the ease of everything that amazed him, the appearance of a butler and a footman with the tea, the informality of Lady Haddalot, who had always lost something and was almost fainting with fatigue, the drinks no one bothered to drink, the French food, the goat's cheese, the pink Chilean wine, the old-looking, immaculate clothes, the coming and going of gardener and chauffeur, the house telephones, the timeless lawn and the dark lake with Hamsyn's white punt. The boathouse was as big as the house where Buck was born, and much more beautiful. He preferred it to the real house, and so did Hamsyn.

'Of course, our house is a bit of a bugger, but I don't mind it.'

'Are you allowed to say bugger?'

'Not to Mummy. But I can to you.'

'Shouldn't you call me "sir"?'

'Christ no. You're only here to teach me Latin.'

'Manners maketh man.'

'Are you a Wykhamist?'

7

'No.'

'Thank God, they're awfully queer. Do you play cricket?'

'Sort of.'

'Good, then you can bowl to me. If you like.'

'I do like.'

I think we shall get on then. What's your name? Is it true you're a famous poet?'

'Not very famous. My name's Buck.'

'What an awfully queer name.'

'So's Hamsyn.'

'That's just in our family. They call me Ham at school.'

'Do you like Ham?'

'God no! I like Hamsyn. I shan't let anyone call me Ham at my public school.'

'How will you stop them?'

'Fight the buggers.'

The drowsy rhythm of the summer took over everything. Even Latin had its rhythm, and the walk to the cricket net became a ritual. The pictures on the study walls became familiar pictures, and the servants became familiar servants. The lime-scented bath before dinner, the whisky before bed, which arrived like the dinner wine in decanters not in bottles, became part of the natural order. But Buck felt he was in Wonderland all the same. His money accumulated because he had nothing to spend it on. But his notebook for new poems accumulated only fragments, because he feared how wealth and unreality might infect his poetry. His serious communication was only with the pictures on the walls, and he noticed that the same seemed to be true of Sir James. Lady Haddalot came to life only at weekends, in a social dexterity which amazed him. Buck began to regret that the summer was not going to last for ever. University summers had been endless, but school summer holidays were short.

Fingest Castle
August 19th

Dear Mike,

How is the novel? Has it got a name yet, because I don't like thinking of it as 'it'? It seems an age since I saw you, and I feel as if all memory of us had been wiped away from our colleges. I find that I left behind half of a pair of shoes in my room, but I shan't go back for it.

Tutoring is an easy life as I always suspected, and I almost wish it would go on for ever. When I have finished I will have saved enough to come to London for a bit, and wondered if I could stay with you? The library here has almost no books about the sex life of the royal family, so I will have to try the BM.

Life in the upper classes is being very funny. It takes five days to get over the weekends, when they swarm like flocks of birds on the lake and playing croquet and cards and baccarat and snooker between dinner bells. There is a daughter who comes who is a snooker champion and is teaching me. She also does gardening before breakfast when the gardener is out of the way, and dances between lunch and tea to v. romantic jazz but I have not fallen. In the winter she shoots foxes or whatever.

I have been thinking of doing a series of parodies of twentieth-century poets and my publisher showed some interest. Shall I or not?

Buck

9

Fingest Castle
September 7th

Dear Mike,

Life has been busy. Last weekend we had a Conservative Fête. All the same, Roy Jenkins came to lunch, and had heard of me. Or was he pretending? Then on Monday there was a frost of all things, and the poor little bastard I teach is going back to school, so the whole house is engaged in packing, including me. The croquet things have been put away in a coffin, and do you know what they do here? They change the curtains for the winter. In every single room. When the p. little b. has been tied up in string and posted off to school, they are all going to Scotland to persecute the stags. I am coming to London, but in fact I will not need to stay with you, not because five in a flat is too many for me, but because I am living with a girl, and she has a flat. She is someone I met here. I don't know if I mentioned her, she plays snooker. She is one of this family but no one seemed to mind us shacking up here, except one night when we missed dinner and they found us in bed. Even then not much. The truth is I have never really enjoyed sex before and she says nor has she: so this may last. Please eat or burn this letter.

You were quite right to have doubts about my parodies. I wrote a few and they went down well here with the guests and Dizzy (the girl) liked them, but the p. little b. was rather scornful and Lady Haddalot said Cecil Day-Lewis wrote better ones! *Day-Lewis*, of all people! But she showed me them and it is true they are far better than mine. So I gnashed my teeth, and now I am not doing any more. See you soon. How's the novel? And how do you like being an ad. man? Successful, I hope.

Buck

P.S. Lady Haddalot is also against my Sex Life of the Royal Family, and as I am cultivating her I feel a bit dissuaded, and must think again or postpone. She wants me to edit the letters home of some dead uncle of hers from 1914. There's money in it, because she would pay, and the book might even sell, so I might do it working here at weekends.

P.P.S. I don't know how to tell my family about this girl, so have decided not to do so. Thank God that Weston-super-Mare is a long way from London.

'He has no money, darling, and no prospect of earning any.'

'How do you know, Mummy?'

'I have a nose for men with no money. Anyway, Hamsyn found out.'

'Little beast. Anyway, Buck's a poet, it's different.'

'They go through money just as quickly as anyone else. Still, I agree it's no obstacle. Your father can look after the money. But what about a career? He won't be happy just living off you and not doing anything.'

'He can do his poetry.'

'Poetry isn't something you do, and a poet isn't something you can be. A man has to have a career as well. Even you have a career.'

'I hate my career. I'd far sooner be a poet's moll than just a model.'

'Moll, Dizzy darling? Has he suggested marriage, darling?'

'Well, mistress then. Muse. Girl. Sheperson. White goddess.'

'Marriage is still a solution, in spite of what people say.'

11

'But Mummy, we're too young to get married. It's just not cool to get married at our age.'

'Well dear, I'll talk to your father about the money. But do consider marriage. You can still have lovers.'

'Oh mummy, what a repellent reason. Anyway, how many lovers have you ever had?'

'More than you imagine, darling. And more than your father imagines.'

'Oh, I say, have you really?'

'Now that's enough, dear. Remember poets are not very faithful. If you want Buck you must find a way of keeping him. I suggest a proper marriage and a proper career, like your father's.'

'But Buck is faithful. Poets are faithful. It's because they're so romantic. That's why I like him.'

'Shakespeare was not very faithful to the Earl of Southampton darling, now was he? I think it's time you drove Hamsyn back to school. You said you would and your car's much bigger than mine.'

'Can I take Buck?'

'Of course you can.'

Buck was not told about this conversation, but he did sense by the evening that some kind of family decision had been taken about him. He was accepted. The subtle process began of binding him down with invisible chains of obligation. Dizzy like her mother was freakishly generous, but her father was formidably and deliberately so. Hamsyn wrote to Buck from school. He found himself taking Lady Haddalot to Sotheby's for her husband's birthday present, meeting the elderly, catlike men of letters of the last generation, and lunching on a lettuce leaf and marmite sandwich with Dizzy at half past three in the afternoon between her London engagements. He began to write again, picking his words like picking his way across a minefield. He took the risk of writing stories, longer poems, childhood memories. Twice he appeared on television, in a show run by someone he met through the Haddalots. They introduced him to Lord Weidenfeld. There seemed no peak he was incapable of climbing, though there were still some he was unwilling to climb.

One day in the early winter she came in rosy-faced from the cold air to find him wrestling with a stanza form based on an Edith Piaf record which he kept playing. It was dusk in the square outside, but he was too preoccupied to draw the curtains or even to turn on the lights. She did it for him, and puffed up the cushions and made tea.

'Darling.'

'Mmm?'

'I brought us a present.'

'Lovely. What?'

'Caviar.'

'Eh?'

'Caviar.'

'Good God. Why?'

'Special reason. Shall I tell you?'

'Mmm. Just let me finish this.'

He was nearly there. He had it right now. The poem only needed words. He kept words in lists. Cabbage. Riviera. Skin. Dung-fire. Linnet. The poem was half-written in his head, so he scribbled a note of it and shut his book.

'Sorry, what? Oh yes, caviar. How nice.'

'There was a reason.'

13

'Someone coming in?'

'No. It's all for us.'

'Oh good. What a big pot.'

'Do you want to know the reason?'

'Of course. Is there one?'

'Yes. Caviar comes from virgin sturgeon.'

'So?'

'Well, it's eggs.'

'Eggs.'

'Virgin sturgeon needs no urgin'! Don't you get it?'

'Not quite.'

'I'm pregnant.'

'Oh my God. Are you sure?'

'Of course I'm sure. I went to the doctor.'

'What shall we do?'

'Have a baby, of course.'

'Oh, my God.'

'Is that all you can say? Oh my God? Don't you want a baby?'

'Yah, er, yep. I mean *our* baby? But we didn't *mean* to, did we? What about your parents?'

He was as white as paper, she was blushing a deeper red and on the edge of tears. They stared at one another.

'What do you mean, we didn't mean to?'

'Well, Catholic girls get pregnant just to make you marry them. It's famous. Look at Fiona.'

'Christ, I hate you sometimes. I knew you were middle class, but I didn't know you could be so common.'

By the end of that interlude several things had been said between them that were unforgivable, and some that the younger reader might think unforgettable. Not so. Memory is effaced by other memory, and the exact

14

record of violently emotional scenes is self-effacing in the course of life. Art is short and pointed, but life is long and pointless. They went through the twists and turns that people go through. Attempted reconciliations made them all the more conscious of the chasm that had opened under their feet. A drink or two heated their words more than it rekindled their affections. They had no appetite for the caviar, but they did eat it, with teaspoons straight out of the pot, as Buck remembered eating cold baked beans at school sitting on his bed.

By the next day Dizzy wanted an abortion but Buck wanted the baby. Their battle of wills ebbed and flowed between them for a week. The weekend took them back to Fingest Castle. Dark clouds leaked rain into the conifers. The punt was put away and the lake was an unrelieved sheet of scarcely gleaming water. Buck stalked around it with mud squelching underfoot, while Dizzy told her mother. News like that causes an immediate splash among one's friends, but few lasting ripples. No one over fifty will be hearing it for the first time. The only way for a coldness to last is if people stop seeing one another, but now Buck and Dizzy felt tied to one another against the world, if only by their quarrel. Sir James was furious at the inefficiency of getting pregnant 'these days, Ha!' Lady Haddalot drew them both into an antechamber of her bedroom during bathtime before dinner, but no heart-to-heart talk took place there, because Hamsyn was home from school and came in search of Buck, and Lord Goodman rang on the house telephone, to say a bath-tap had come off in Stephen Spender's hand. They agreed to meet again later.

15

But after dinner Buck formally proposed marriage, first to Sir James over the brandy, then to Lady Haddalot over the *petit point* in a corner of the drawing room, and finally to Dizzy, whom he ran to earth watching a video of *Blackadder* in the television room with Hamsyn. Hamsyn had done sufficiently well in Common Entrance to get into Eton, so he was pleased with himself, and Sir James was grateful to the tutor.

'Not much of a career, Ha! Still, you're good at it, that shows. You could become a beak, I suppose?'

'Or a novelist.'

'No, no. Worse than a poet. What about Parliament, ha? Sound views, I suppose? Not that that matters, ha! Still, no hurry.'

Dizzy had her abortion all the same. She was prepared to marry Buck, so she said, but not yet, and not to bear this child. She went on modelling; Buck moved out into a flat Sir James had found for him, and began to be groomed for a south-coast constituency where the MP was so doddering that his head might fall off at any time. His retirement to the House of Lords was attractive to himself and a relief to his colleagues. But there was a snag. The Conservative Party, having suffered scandals of every other kind short of treason, was determined to insure against any more sex. Buck had to go before a selection committee of the Central Office at the Holiday Inn, Slough. They liked him being all the things he was, a writer from a minor public school, and the son of a dead vicar whose widow worked as a lady dentist in Weston-super-Mare. His connections and references were good. He had done well in his school debating society and the Union, and never bothered to join the Communist Party.

But he was unmarried, and in 1985, fear and horror of sexual scandal being what it was among Conservatives, only married men could pass. Buck pleaded his engagement, but they told him it had never been announced. He promised to announce it at once, so on that condition they passed him. For Dizzy this manoeuvre was the last straw. It was at the Holiday Inn, Slough, that he really lost her.

The Haddalots chilled him slowly and painlessly. Buck never knew who got him his jobs and his contracts. He never had known and did not know now how much or little interest Sir James took in him. By the time of the Holiday Inn fiasco he was too closely interwoven into the family's schemes and its social circle to be dropped without loss of face to them. The letters from the dead uncle were in the press, and both as a tutor and a suitor, Buck had become a fixture at Fingest weekends. People expressed mild surprise that they never saw him in Scotland or in Switzerland. He already had experience of other houses, other woods and parks, as a member of the Haddalot retinue. Servants recognized him, and he knew which ones to tip. Lady Haddalot told him that, the day she observed him frisking up to an old gardener at Chatsworth to offer him a five pound note. But Buck had friends of his own among the friends of friends. It was rumoured that the wife of an elderly courtier, a lady old enough to be his mother, had found him amusing and useful and was taking him in hand. People like to believe the worst about relationships, but people are sometimes wrong.

'His mother, darling, is a puller of teeth in Weston-super-Mare. He must be after the gold fillings in

Anastasia's teeth.'

'A funny way to get at her teeth. How do you know about the mother?'

'Dizzy Haddalot told Robert.'

'Oh?'

'And Robert told Hugh, of course, and Hugh told me.'

'Hugh's such a liar. I wonder if it's true?'

'I checked with Dizzy.'

'Gosh, you are daring.'

Buck knew his way around people like this better than he knew it around London. They entertained him, and he wrote about them in crowded notebooks. All you had to do was to alter the names and the backgrounds and you could put them into poems. He was working on a long sequence of sonnets about sexual snobbery in the African slave trade in the nineteenth century, entirely based on the richest white women he knew. The physical details of his Africa came from French travel writers and the amazing store rooms of the Museum of Mankind at the back of Burlington House. He had acquired a taste for nourishing bric-à-brac early in life, on summer holidays when it always rained, in tiny museums at Lyme Regis and Bembridge and Portland Bill. The Museum of Mankind was his climax of pleasures, his refuge from life, and the title of his second collection of poems.

Inwardly and secretly, he grieved for his Dizzy, and over his lost child. The centre of his grief was an emptiness which he defended. He resented her, he needed her, he wrote her off, he thought about her always. It infuriated him to realize she had been right so many times. He tried to live by other standards, but always returned to hers. Seen through hindsight, that first summer at Fingest when he drifted into an affair without knowing where he was headed, assuming somehow that love had no consequences, or that love never arose from sex, was like a perfect time to him, a favourite film. He remembered the drifting of the punt and the downwards drifting of the sun. If his affliction had been a few degrees worse, he would have taken to asthma, become Proust. But he was not so deep a character, not so overwhelming an ego. The Museum of Mankind was too fascinating. It was always closing time there, but the social life of London kept him afloat.

Dizzy was not grieving for Buck, and the thought of her lost baby flung her into such a panic that she dared not brood over it. She had loved Buck more the more she saw of him, much more in London than at Fingest, where to start with he was only an unexpected weekend amusement, but more than ever when they went together as guests to other people's houses, and slipped away alone into empty rooms. For Dizzy those hiding-places were a fresh reliving of the intimate secrecies and the deadly seriousness of childhood. But now she loved him less for seeing him less, her life was full and he had gone from it and been replaced. When she thought of him at all she blamed him and hated him. When she spoke about him to her new lover, who was an aspiring film director, she exaggerated Buck's faults until he sounded so monstrous that the filmic lover lost interest in him even as a rival, even as a joke. But she kept the abortion to herself.

198, Inkerman Road,
Fulham

Dear Mike,

Having no phone here yet I thought I would write, so that you are the first to know my new address. There has been a bit of a row about my new book, *Museum of Mankind*, which you may have seen. One of my African slave ladies says some things that I really took from the lips of an old trout called Lady Bott, and someone (Dizzy?) has told her, and she looks like sueing. I denied it to the publisher, natch, but now there is talk of witnesses, and I seem to have been incredibly indiscreet. Please nail all rumours.

Anyway at the moment I am living in Fulham and phoneless. It is a nice quiet neighbourhood with a few friendly Asians and some retired firemen from the Battle of Britain in braces. You can park a car here though they get vandalized overnight someone said. I will stay here until the fuss dies down, may keep it on for a secret work place for ever, as the phone is always ringing at home.

I have a chance of a job at the TV Centre working on a new documentary series. It would fit well with my poems at present, they are veering that way. No chance of their doing the Sex Life of the Royal Family alas, but I suppose that was a bit of a cheeky idea. Actually just before this row I had met the Queen Mother and she was as sweet as apple pie and cream, she really was. Just like everyone says. It rather rules out that book, and anyway if La Bott brings an action I don't expect any publisher will touch me for some time.

Glad to hear your novel is going well. Do not worry about me. I think the worst that will happen is I'll be cut at the races or something. I already find it quite hard to avoid the places Dizzy goes, but after this I will have to draw a circle round myself and live inside that. Do you ever have lunch, non-liquid I mean? My club, Tuesday, 12.30 for 1? Or if you hate clubs we could meet at the Museum of Mankind, same day and time. Let me know.

Buck

With a friend like Mike you did not need any enemies. On the day after their lunch, a full account of it, with plenty about Lady Bott and the outraged publisher and the poet's desert island in Fulham, figured in a gossip column. The evening papers picked up the story, the next day it was news not gossip, and Lady Bott made a statement to the press. Buck found his own face, startled but elegant like the White Rabbit's, staring greyly out of the newsprint. A letter from home expressed fury at the persecution of his mother and aunts by a local journalist.

It all died down quite suddenly of course, but meanwhile the book sold and his reputation sank among the serious-minded. He was sneered at in little magazines, attacked on the radio by *Critics' Forum*, and defended in *Marxism Today*. His poems had to be reprinted. On a weekend when Dizzy was away, Lady Haddalot asked him back to Fingest.

He went in his little green second-hand sports car, threading his way between the beech trees, into the silence of the park, past the goats and the view of the lake, into the shadow of the same old casual, confident house. He glanced anxiously at the bigger, sleeker cars of the other guests. But he was greeted as a conquering hero. The butler creaked his mouth open smiling, and twinkled his eyes. The footman nodded and grinned as friend to friend. Buck had given his tips the last time in just the correct proportions, but doubling the amounts. With the family and his fellow-guests he had learnt in the same way to expend energy in the proper proportion but in twice the usual quantity, which made him a most desirable visitor to all concerned.

Sometimes the people the Haddalots asked for the weekend were named after county towns, Sophie Dorchester and Daphne Winchester, sometimes after London Square, Lord Eaton, James Belgrave, Charles St James, and sometimes after entire counties. 'Do you know North Riding?' 'Let me introduce you to the Border Counties.' The famous ones were easiest, because they were the true aristocracy of the weekends, while the ones with the county names were the plebs of these occasions, unless of course they were established and famous at once, like Lord Harlech or Lord Home, who seldom saw the Haddalots. Buck discovered that his quarrel with Lady Bott had done him nothing but good. He had reached the ranks of the socially famous, from which heights he could peer down on the bald heads of the establishment for as long as his fame lasted.

'Buck, I hear everyone's crowding to get into your poems.'

'What was it like in Fulham?'

'I thought that horrible Elspeth Bott deserved all she got.'

'Did you see her cartoon in *Private Eye*?'

'Did you see it in *The Times*?'

'Did you see what Ali Forbes wrote in the *Spectator*?'

'Do you think it dished your chances for Parliament?'

'Change parties, old boy, that's what I did.'

'Change clubs, old boy, nobody would have minded at White's.'

'Change publishers. George Weidenfeld is longing to publish you.'

'Of course he doesn't do much poetry.'

'Of course they don't have a lot of poets.'

'Of course you still have to find a constituency.'

'George could arrange something, or at least I'm sure Jasper could, and they're as thick as thieves. Jasper could ask Victor. Come to that I could ask Victor myself, if I ever saw him.'

There was a deeper reason than this frothy conversation, which moved so easily between mocking affection and not quite affectionate mockery, for his invitation to Fingest. Lady Haddalot was seriously worried about Dizzy. The aspiring film-maker had stopped aspiring to make films. He had begun to speak of transcendent experiences and bought a set of finger-bells. Cinnamon-flavoured smoke wafted through Dizzy's flat: it was thought to disguise a coarser, more dangerous smell.

'Last weekend,' said Lady Haddalot, 'her bedroom here stank like a fox's earth. I couldn't let the maids go into it. I'm at my wit's end, Buck. I look to you.'

'It's painful for me too.'

'Of course it is, because you love her. Will you still marry her?'

'What?'

'She loves you. You're the clue. I'm sure of it. If we get rid of this wretched man, if she agrees, I want you to marry her. I'm sure she can be saved.'

23

'Get rid of him how?'

'Pay him off.'

'What?'

'Leave it to Sir James, Buck dear. He has experience of these things.'

'How?'

'Well, he might finance the film, you see.'

'Did he dare ask him to? It's millions to finance a film.'

'The idea was floating round the City. The important thing is to rescue Dizzy, and you are Sir Galahad.'

'Sir Tristram, more like. I drank the magic potion.'

'Had you slept with a sword between you, we should never have had this trouble. Will you now marry Dizzy or will you not?'

'Yes. Yes. Yes. Er – I mean if . . .'

'If what, Buck?'

'If she wants me.'

'Oh, you poet! Don't you understand anything?'

'Not really.'

'The film-maker's queer, gay, whatever you call it. She's living as a lesbian and taking drugs and has to be rescued.'

'How do you know?'

'On the best authority.'

Fingest Castle

Dear Mum,

I thought I ought to tell you I am getting married. It was all arranged extremely quickly in the end or I would have told you. We are getting married tomorrow privately in the village. We have known each other quite

24

a long time, and were engaged once before but never fixed a date, but this time I am being more businesslike and have nailed her down.

This address is her parents' place, she is called Diana (Dizzy) Haddalot, I met her when I was a tutor to her brother. It is not a castle really, but a house in a park with a lake. There are some goats you would like.

We are honeymooning in America and will send a card. If writing, use this address for now. I have got a new job in the Conservative Central Office in Public Relations.

Best love

Buck

P.S. Could you go on storing Dad's books for me until we get settled?

The wedding was neither private nor uneventful. Dizzy was cold and straight and pale in a defiant white dress from Paris, her friend in sin sulked behind a pillar in furious bright green, her mother was warm and weepy in gauzes, Sir James gave her away with parade-ground alacrity. The vicar, whom Buck had never seen before, snapped his teeth together and grinned; he said in his sermon how good it was to see young people so devout, and how as a member of the area team ministry he always liked marriages because they meant more communicants. He said if Jesus spoke English he would have called marriage the supreme example of planned giving in every sense.

Dizzy let Buck kiss her at the reception, but she danced

with him like an Infanta of Spain, not as she used to dance to her old jazz. Maybe she was thinking of her dress. Hoping to conciliate Dizzy, Buck danced with her lesbian friend, who was slightly drunk, but otherwise just like anyone else. She was called Sandy. She and Buck got on well, because he found her a bottle of whisky which she hid in a flower-pot for refills instead of champagne. She poured him some as well, and as the evening went on he returned to her corner at shorter and shorter intervals. The reception pursued its organized course to nowhere like a slow train of first-class carriages. For Dizzy it was a night train where you wake to see the Balkans and the snow. She took cocaine in the Ladies, having saved some up, but it helped less than usual. Buck she could stand, now that she was seeing him again; it was her mother she hated. It was good to see Buck getting on with Sandy. What on earth was that they were drinking? Thank God Sandy was coming on the honeymoon.

When the time came for bride and groom to leave for their Secret Destination, which was an airport hotel at Heathrow, neither of them found it easy to walk, but they were bundled somehow into the car, and off they trundled, with one of Hamsyn's football boots tied to the rear bumper. Sandy followed after a discreet interval. Her capacity for whisky was nearly infinite, so she drove herself quite sedately, stopping only twice under dark hedges for a pull from her private bottle, to the music of her favourite tape. That was Provençal shepherd songs from the fourteenth century, with a lot of calling out and sheep noises and bird noises.

They travelled in a huge canoe down a long river in

the Yellowstone National Park, ten days of brainless beauty and infinite air, infinite forest. No one in London realizes there still are such places on earth. At night they slept like children in one big bag they called the dream-bag. At one time or another, each of them had sex with each of the others, out of sudden hunger but without rapture. Buck began to think well of himself, physically, intellectually and morally, but Dizzy and Sandy felt closer linked than ever before; he became their cook, their map-reader, their appendage. When they got to New York, a different and more dangerous split developed in their small society. Had they travelled down American rivers for ever, they might have stayed together for ever, but a relationship that can defy convention may still be unable to stand up to the pressures and opportunities of New York.

Sandy began to foster the poetry while Dizzy ignored it. 'How can I describe common garden flowers without their names?' he would ask. 'Common flowers? Does that convey anything, Alexandra?' 'Common garden flowers without names,' she would answer. 'Brilliant,' he said, 'it's iambic.' 'Christ, how silly you two are,' said Dizzy. In a day or two Buck noticed she was taking drugs again. After a week he lost her altogether for twenty-four hours. She came home to the hotel looking terrible and penniless. Sometimes he thought Sandy was as frightened as he was, but at other times he was sure she was conniving. There was nothing he could do and no one he could turn to.

He lived out the last day or two of his honeymoon in a state of jitters. Dizzy was more tranquil, she appeared to have come through a crisis, though the habit of vanishing for hours at a time and returning in an odd state remained with her. She showed alarming interest in religion, for the first time in Buck's experience of her. She probed him about his dead religious father, bought oriental bangles from what looked like the freakiest surviving mystic in Manhattan, and dressed Sandy in a garland of expensive flowers, though that gesture might have been intended to drown a smell of pot that was making itself felt again. 'It comes from the ventilators of every hotel in New York,' she said when Buck remarked on it, 'like Legionnaires' Disease. It's the servants.'

She must have spent more money than anyone knew in New York. It was a mystery where she got so much. The package of cocaine they found in Buck's case at Heathrow had what the customs men called a 'street value' of a million. The consequences were nasty, brutish, and prolonged. All three of them were taken to ominous little examination rooms and most rudely searched. Buck of course claimed he knew nothing about the package. His fingerprints were not on it. 'But that might just be your cunning, sir, mightn't it?' The two girls were let out in the end, but Buck was taken away to Brixton, up the hill between the trees and the seedy hotels, along the lane under the old brick wall, and in through the slammed gates to the prison courtyard where the prize Alsatian dogs sat like sentries.

It was made clear to Buck by a lawyer that he ought to plead guilty. No doubt his youth and promise and clean character would earn him a light sentence. But there was such a lot of the stuff. Bail was refused, and he began to get used to the deadly routines of prison. The worst part of it was the noise of the other prisoners at night, and the smell in the early morning. Otherwise prison was much like school, same food, same faces, similar architecture, the same aching and aching for a letter from home, for a visit. Buck had no visitors and very few letters, none from Dizzy except one that the chaplain delivered personally, saying it was a 'Dear John' and sitting with him while he read it. She was divorcing him, that was what that meant. Buck's mother's letter was far more painful, being all about how his 'dear father' was lucky to be dead, and why could Buck not have studied something sensible at college, like dentistry. Sandy sent postcards.

'They teach you to ski now with tiny skis like toothpicks so I have been swooping about this mountain. Dizzy swift and perfect but I will catch her up. Hope jug is not horrid. Are you a tobacco baron? Love, Sandy.'

'We are in this unaltered hotel where Proust stayed aged twelve. Food smooth, *longueurs* deadly, nothing to do but gamble. Dizzy's new religion is casinos. Betted a lot in your name and you won nearly a hundred pounds not francs. How is jug? Can you take 'A' levels? Try carpentry. Love, Sandy.'

Buck went through the usual three stages of new prisoners, first the shock and paralysis, then the frantic struggling and impotent attempt to fight his case, and finally the bowing of the head and waiting for the days to pass. One of the screws advised him to learn a foreign language. 'I've learnt Polish since I've been working here,' he said, 'and Hungarian. Very nice holidays I've had there.' 'I've been to Hungary,' said Buck, 'I hated it.' It was some time before he came up for sentence, in fact he had been in prison so long that a court appearance already seemed like an outing to the seaside. The judge looked like a pleasant old buzzard, and the lawyers all seemed confident. Everyone said Buck had been used. Dizzy stepped into the witness box and said it was the first experience of New York that undid him. She was dignified and white-faced and said she was divorcing him. She never looked at him. He got two years, because the judge was inclined to believe he was simple, but not all that innocent.

Dartmoor prison was built as an experimental agricultural centre by the Prince Regent; it did not take long to prove by experiment that the place was too bleak and too wild for agriculture. The older prison buildings were built for American prisoners in the war of 1812 and French Napoleonic prisoners. Seen from a distance they have a certain stark nobility, and the moor itself stretches away like a petrified cloud formation in every direction. Buck liked it, and found the other prisoners excellent company. He was sent to Dartmoor because it was near his mother, who was the only known good influence on him, but she said she was busy as a dentist, and never did visit him on the Moor. Indeed, she could never hear it mentioned without a shudder, ever again. She counted Buck as dead for the rest of her life; if he ever sent a Christmas card she kept it hidden.

'Came here to get away from Christmas, but failed. Bright silver and gold decorations strung between lampposts in blazing sun, v. odd effect, and mechanical frogs hop on every pavement. Parthenon smells of petrol. Dizzy has become very pro-Turkish, and wants to go on to Istanbul where the frogs are real. Off now to seaside for a gamble in your name. Hope Dartmoor view amusing. Love, Sandy.'

He made a number of interesting acquaintances in prison, but no deep or lasting friends. He found life without women more boring than he would have expected, and the male tarts were like German Expressionists' parodies of male tarts. The sexual offenders were locked up in a wing on their own for fear of being molested by the aggressively 'normal' prisoners. Everything about Dartmoor suggested a working-class public school of illiberal tendency: except for the inmates of course. Buck was what commercial travellers call a good mixer, and was not unpopular even with the screws, except for the one he snubbed at Brixton about learning Hungarian, and the head chaplain at Dartmoor who was an ex-paratrooper and hated slackness and decadence.

He worried about his poetry. He did scribble a few verses, not as yuppy as before but more bodyline, towards a collection called *Green Bottles*, because green medicine bottles used to contain poison; he remembered some at home that disappeared at the time of his father's heart attack. He pondered the possibilities of suicide and murder, but in the end he confined those to metaphors, and the collection when it appeared was called *Heart Attack*. He wrote nothing about prison itself: that was a numb time. Poetry colonized it only as some self-generated weed spreads across an unplanted plot of earth. He lost his remission and never saw a parole board, because he refused all co-operation with the Governor, the Social Workers, and so on. He expressed no contrition, offered no explanations, and refused to discuss what he called his private affairs.

'The Governor,' he said to another prisoner at exercise, 'is a creep.'

'Things are getting worse and worse.'

'Mailbags aren't what they were.'

'Nor are shoeboxes.'

'Do we make shoeboxes?'

'No, if we did they'd be better made. Work's so slovenly outside.'

'Yes.'

'Shoeboxes used to be so big and well made.'

'I suppose they did.'

'Now they're too small for the shoes.'

'Are they? I never noticed.'

'Nor did I, until I came to cut up that woman. I left pieces of her all over London, you may have heard about it.'

'I believe I did.'

'They'd never have caught me, but it took such a long time and such a lot of shoeboxes. If they were bigger like they used to be, they'd never have caught me.'

'So you're another Conservative voter.'

'Of course. Who isn't? Creeps like the bloody governor.'

Buck got out of prison two years older, but no wiser, and no more employable than before. The social worker asked him if he had a job to go to, and he replied, without thinking, the Conservative Central Office. He was reported for cheek. Still, he had his self-respect as a poet, and found to his delight that quite a serious sum of money was being kept for him in a Swiss bank account as a result of Sandy's gambling. But he had no address for her. The last postcard had been a picture of London, but it said: 'We are still moving about a lot.' Buck was quite free, divorced and socially ruined and free, almost perfectly friendless and free.

He spent several weeks doing the sort of things one wants to do after years of imprisonment. He stayed in a cool, expensive room in a hotel, ate stupefying meals, took over his house in Fulham which had been let, repaired it and cut back its shaggy garden. He went on journeys, got a new passport, wandered about late at night. He behaved in fact much more suspiciously than he ever had done in his life before. One morning two detectives called.

'We felt that the truth never came out lad, at your trial. We could of course search your house. We could search you now. We'd find something sooner or later, so why not avoid the inconvenience? What we want is names. Where did it come from, where was it going to? It can't have *all* been for your own use, now can it?'

'I don't have to talk to you, do I?'

'You don't *have* to but . . . think of the inconvenience. You don't want to go back inside.'

'No.'

'Was what you said actually true? You just brought it across for a man who said his sister would collect it? A man you never saw before?'

'Yes.'

'But when you were first arrested, lad, you said you knew nothing about it. That was acting guilty. Why did you do that? Was it true?'

'I just said what came into my head.'

'We shall be keeping an eye on you, lad.'

Fortunately for Buck, he led them to no dangerous

trails, or none more dangerous than Dizzy's. She telephoned him late at night from a house in Wales. She was rambling and almost incoherent, she wept, she repeated herself, she wandered away from the phone to get a drink and he heard her dropping something. She was less than clear about her own address. But she wanted him, at once or sooner, so they made a plan to meet at a country hotel that squatted among coniferous trees beside the gloomiest reservoir in Wales. Buck had never heard of it but Dizzy seemed to know it well. He found that strange, because it could scarcely be a casino, though gambling seemed to be her craze. He could not imagine the Dizzy he knew weeping her way hysterically around a succession of Welsh fishing hotels. What was the attraction of Wales for her? Did she feel at home with the architecture and the goats?

He suspected Dizzy was taking heroin. She was certainly drinking a lot. Sandy was her minder and her tea-maker and perhaps her guru. They both gambled and they both drank, and they were like two people drowning by clutching one another too tightly. But there was no regular pattern about their life, they had their good weeks and good seasons of the year. Buck never knew where the heroin came from, any more than he ever understood the truth about the cocaine. Several explanations were possible, he mulled them over but came to no conclusion. At first he thought Dizzy was drinking from remorse or despair; he suggested a doctor, but that idea was greeted with stony looks.

'She's got a doctor,' said Sandy.

'A shrink?'

'He specializes in our trouble.'

'What trouble?'

'Addictions.'

A syringe was in the bathroom. The bottles were in the bedroom. The gambling seemed to be dormant. Buck soon got over his initial shock. Dizzy had certainly gone downhill, but he thought she had become a nicer person, more herself. She dried her tears and combed her hair for him, and they went for an evening walk up the mountainside, through a cloud of gnats, then high up into purer, chillier air and the last sun, an isolated world of sheep and grass and big rocks with patches of heather. Miles away across the lake, from some chance fold of the mountainside, you could hear a train, echoing and echoing. They were happy again together. In a way that first week at the hotel was like Yellowstone over again. Buck stopped thinking about prison, Sandy lost her look of wary possessiveness and relaxed again, Dizzy started to paint tight little pictures, using only a thumb and a kitchen knife, and always in one colour, on pieces of cardboard and the torn covers of books. They were happy together as if they had a future.

All the same, several things were different about their lives. They had moved outside the world of Fingest, so that Dizzy's parents spoke of her in vaguely amused, vaguely painful terms, as so many of the other parents they knew spoke of children that had travelled the same path. There were no more suggestions of careers, or of a lapse that could be covered over. Dizzy was more serious, except for those days when she gave up altogether. Sandy was more thoughtful, poking at the lake water with a stick as if she might uncover the ruined villages that it had flooded. Buck's mood was sombre because he thought more bad news was to come. He had smelt the mythical place where storms are brewed or born, or he had discerned the flicker of paranoia in the eye of the Buddha. Whenever he thought of the future, he was frightened out of his wits, so he tried not to do so.

Sometimes they talked about going away together, all three of them, to settle in Rhodes or in Mexico. They thought of a crofter's life in Scotland, but it was too tough; a writers' commune at Cuernaco, or an artists' colony somewhere in Spain. Sandy took to playing on a small wooden recorder by the lakeside or high up in the mountains, while Dizzy just lay and listened, and Buck read his way for the third or fourth time through a disintegrating paperback anthology of American poetry. He was trying to change his style again, but the ghosts of old poems hemmed him in, poems not written or stillborn. In a month they had moved no further than some steep little green hills near Malvern where Dizzy acquired a cottage which was really a gardener's hut. Here they cooked for themselves on a gas ring, here they went quietly to seed, here they were pinned down by a doleful brown dog they called Pollution that they bought from a gipsy. Pollution had an enchanting howl whenever he heard the recorder, but he was smelly by habit and buried his bones until they were rank. He was an amateur of middens and an archaeologist of dustbins.

Sometimes their small family increased for a time, when a stray acquaintance became a guest; some of them stayed for weeks. The summer mouldered on, smelling of foxes, the guests slept a lot and the dog lay gently stinking. Breakfast and lunch scarcely occurred, but supper lasted for hours and hours until the bottles

stood empty, or the most troublesome of the guests had
to be put outside or persuaded to bed. Pollution lay
watching the end of every evening with a stare of never-
ending curiosity. When dawn came he would frisk off
into the allotments at a kind of lolloping trot, hoping to
catch the laziest of birds. One of the visitors was an ex-
hippy called Augustine or Gus, who was an old flame of
Sandy's, and a fan of Buck's, two facts which Buck found
equally upsetting. Gus wrote long poems about Pollution, poems about their life, and an absolutely terrible
poem about the allotments, which Buck found it hard to
praise, and yet he could hardly bear not to return praise
for the praise he was always receiving. The ex-hippy had
a kind of diluted form of hippy wisdom or folk wisdom,
but he was unattractive, and Buck thought he was a
drug-pusher. In fact he was very tiresome indeed. But he
was the lamest duck in sight, and Dizzy fell for him. That
was how the summer ended. When it was over it seemed
like just an episode to all three of them, almost like an
episode that had never happened.

If this book were Buck's autobiography, those weeks
would scarcely figure in it. Their essence would hardly
flavour one paragraph. He would have collapsed them
into how he felt when he came out of prison. But they
affected his poems, his style loosened out and he began to
have a small, intoxicating critical importance. He began
to read the papers and magazines, and to write in them,
and that of course drew him to London, where he might
well have settled down earlier. It drew him to a different
kind of life. Maybe he was so tired of things as they were
that he was weary of his own prolonged and luxuriating
weariness, like Sir Henry Bishop's lark: 'Lo hear the

gentle lark, weary of rest. . . .' Maybe he was pregnant with poetry. He was not at all tired of Dizzy, or of Sandy, only of that life. They all thought they would meet again quite soon.

PART TWO

The oomph had gone out of Buck's life all the same, and he drifted into advertising as a broken pram might drift into a puddle. The miracle was that the pram floated and the puddle seemed just for a moment to be as wide as the Atlantic sea. He was particularly good at advertising cigarettes: he invented 'Sebastian Coe is secretly longing for a fag', and George V lighting a fag-end for a dying soldier, and Mrs Thatcher taking a light from Britannia, and W.G. Grace saying 'I never read government health warnings'. He found that sort of thing easy, providing he was not asked to take it seriously, which ruled him out for most agencies, so he worked in some crumbling wooden offices somewhere at the back of Bond Street, in a sub-unit of an out-unit of a rich agency. His career as a copywriter had a wobble when he lost the Hovis account with a joke about growing bread from packets which nobody understood. But he came back fighting with a TV banking ad about the cherry on the cake, and the cherry on the icing on the cake.

In a way he seemed to himself a paradigm of how the nineteen-sixties led to the nineteen-eighties, and of what a sad story that was. It was the kind of perspective advertising people liked to have. His consolations for exile from the mainstream of the business were his tea lady, an elderly Cockney who loved him and whom he loved and studied, and the fact that at least the more sophisticated agencies had given up talking about creativity, though he believed there was still a man at J. Walter Thompson with Director of Creation written up on his door, and the idea of being creative still darkly flourished in sixth forms and provincial parsonages. Creativity was a ghostly idea, and Buck was too clever to entertain it, though he was not all that clever. Poets are not all that clever. Still, he had a sense of salvation, inherited no doubt from the meagre livelihoods of his ancestors: whatever he earned at this time he banked and forgot, and whatever he learned he lavished only on his poetry, never directly on his life.

He began to have a routine, like most Londoners. His lodgings were at first somewhere to the north-east of Shakespeare's London, in one of the numerous Maiden Lanes where flathats, which in those days meant apprentices, used to stare at the mysteries, as the maidens were named still more recently. Buck became a master of the Underground, though he never came to control the bus routes, so his journey to work included quite long walks at both ends. The difference between Aldgate and Aldgate East was impressed on him by a very long walk at two in the morning. Day by day he came to know certain plane trees, part of the groaning, scattered forest of London, and then to notice certain window boxes, certain peculiar alliances of architecture, a bank with red terracotta foliage and a bakery with spoilt Victorian windows, a corner for finding a taxi, and another less favoured, indeed wholly unfavourerd corner, which he disliked because of a persistent smell of oil and stagnant water from the docks. He was amazed by the variety and local warmth of London, the enormous, meaninglessly ornamented old buildings that might equally be flats or offices, the incoherent, trickling energy of the place. Like more than 90 per cent of Londoners, he felt an outsider in more than 90 per cent of London. Within his routine he felt only relatively at home.

Things were a little better when he moved to one of the bushiest roads in Ealing, to a flat in a house that had linoleum on the stairs and a streetlight that shone through the leaves of a dark green tree into his bedroom. He bought his own furniture, a haphazard collection ranging from nineteen-fifties utility to Victorian baroque. He ate out usually in central London. Life was a prolonged entertainment of clients and colleagues, ham and eggs in Shepherd's Market, Buck's fizz in the office, tinned whisky cake, oysters at Wheeler's, dinner at any of nine restaurants in Mount Street, seven of them owned by the same bright-eyed Italian chef. He kept accounts at great hotels and lost account of money. He wooed a Dr Fürer for the Nestlé's chocolate account, with 'Nestlés for nestlings', but this failed to please. He wooed the Guinness account with 'Guinness is bad for you', but that was thought to be a downmarket joke, and Guinness was aiming upmarket. Dr Fürer toyed for a time with 'Nestlé's is wicked', and Guinness would have liked to market 'Baby Guinness for the very young', or even 'Guinness for nursing mothers', but readers will not be surprised to hear that many of Buck's efforts came to nothing. What was called a concept was usually slow to emerge; he was restless, and they thought him bizarre. The big prize in that business was to become an account director, in control of a huge amount of other people's money, but that dignity eluded him. He was tolerated as a house jester, and as a poet, but only tolerated.

The time was ripe for Buck to meet Loftus. Loftus had a stake in the agency, and he favoured people like Buck. When other advertisers such as Buck's friend Mike held whoopee in public houses that overflowed onto the pavements of mewses on the stroke of opening time, or in wine bars where no one else ever seemed to set foot, Loftus held court in the downstairs bar at the Ritz among mahogany panelling where a few peaceful waiters skimmed like swallows, and in later years, after the Ritz changed hands, in a Victorian hotel near Westminster, which he called 'the Conservative Party at prayer old man, it impresses the foreign johnnies: frightens all hell out of me'. Loftus had a mysterious private business in vintage aeroplanes. He was said to have fought his way through the Battle of Britain in Hurricanes wearing carpet slippers and paying for his own aircraft. 'Wonderful war old fruit, would have paid to join in, wouldn't you?' All the same, on Yom Kippur he could not be found except in the Synagogue behind the Cumberland Hotel . Loftus was a figure of myth. He was suspected to be an armaments dealer, but his own right hand had no idea into what dish his left hand dipped.

Loftus liked to meet the coming young men in the agency. He put opportunities in their way, and benignly wrote down their failures to his own experience. He was anxious about Buck because he sensed a downward turn in the graph of his poetic production. 'Plenty of time, old boy, plenty of time. Doesn't do to rush it. Still, one doesn't want to miss the fun of life, does one? Poetry's your fun I dare say, as flying was mine.'

'Yes,' said Buck, 'no, one doesn't want to lose it,'

easing himself uncomfortably into his leather chair. 'Do you still fly?'

'Oh yes, I race a bit, but there aren't so many races now. Raced round the Isle of Wight the other day. Potty easy.'

'Where did you come?'

'Oh first, old boy. No point in not coming first, I mean is there? But about this poetry . . .' It was partly from self-respect, partly to try out some new work, and partly to get Loftus off his back that Buck agreed to give a reading at the Poetry Society.

He knew little about this organization except that people seemed to despise it, but his publisher begged him to accept the invitation, and Loftus was pleased when he did. It is hard to know how or by what stages Loftus attained such influence over Buck. It was not just his money or his myth, his crinkly face or his mad-looking blue eyes or white moustache, but all these things. It was the unlikeliness of his pleasures and the unexpected common sense of his critical views. It was even his personal smell, compounded of brandy, tweed, cigars and expensive hair lotion. Very expensive indeed, considering he had so little hair. Before either of them knew it, Loftus had become to Buck a kind of father figure. He brooded over the boy's divorce, and over his future. Buck found himself devoting more and more energy to pleasing old Loftus, both at business and outside business. Loftus had a family that Buck had never met, in the rich humus of the Surrey hills, but the mystery of Loftus was part of his attraction. The unknown areas of his life drew you on.

Loftus provoked young men to a gentle rivalry;

something inside him was 'silent upon a peak in Darien', which they would never attain. Buck had just had the walls of his office covered with all the pages of the London Telephone Directory, glued and varnished. This idea was adapted from a room at Rydal Mount that Wordsworth's sister Dorothy papered with *The Times*: Buck was proud of it. Loftus just grunted. His own office walls were covered with very expensive chintz. 'Rather a fussy pattern if you look closely,' he complained of the numbers. 'Lionel Johnson used grey parcel paper, if you must behave like a poet.'

'Not chintz in the nineties?' Buck asked him.

'Flaubert used chintz,' said Loftus, 'in the eighteen-sixties. Degas used yellow handkerchiefs.'

On the evening of the poetry reading they met at a new rendezvous, an extremely modern and expensive-looking yacht club on the edge of Kensington beside the Hyde Park Hotel. 'Easy to get a taxi from here, young poet,' said Loftus. 'Glass of wine?'

By the time they got to the peeling square in Earls Court where Buck was meant to read, he was not sure whether he was drunk or terrified; he thought terror predominated. The taxi had difficulty finding the place, in spite of having its address. It was like a seedy if dignified lodging house where Indian students might be living in hope of a cheque from home, or where a professor's daughter who prowled the streets and the museums all day might spend half the night writing pages of brilliant diary destined to oblivion. There was a library downstairs, or as it turned out a bookshop, devoted to poetry as Church bookshops are devoted to religion. Buck was alarmed to see a poster with his name on it, though it was not the only poster. A girl who seemed to be running the whole sad world of poetry in London apologized that they had none of his books. 'Your publisher is bringing them himself,' she said. 'We hope you might be called on to sign some. OK? Would you like a drink through there?'

Buck clutched for a glass of 'Red or white?' and stared at the walls, which were decorated with poster verses in pink handwriting on dark blue. One was about the bomb and one was about vasectomy, and one was about children playing with little lambs. The room began to fill with people, Loftus was lost, someone gave Buck a third or a fourth drink. He spotted a young man he thought he remembered from the Ealing train, but it was a poet from Wimbledon. A couple of uncertain sex but amazing beauty in lookalike black and silver clothes and Scandinavian wigs nodded to him, but smiled only at one another. He was introduced to a famous black activist whose name he never caught. His publisher pushed towards him, waving books and pen over his head. He caught a glimpse of Loftus in the distance with some people from the office. He had to find the gents. Loftus, he felt feebly, would know where it was.

'Er – we're about ready I think, if you'd like to start.'

As he stood at last in the gents, relieving his body but not his soul, and cooling his head on the wall, Buck heard a familiar voice.

'Hi, man.'

Buck went dumb with displeasure and panic.

'Hi, you remember me? Gus? That cottage in the Malverns with the two girls? Wow, were they something!'

'How did you find me?'

'Come to hear your stuff, man.'

'How did you hear about this?'

'Oh the grapevine. Posters and stuff. I'm in this very cultural squat now, behind Islington Public Library.'

'You left Dizzy?'

'Sandy slung me out.'

'Oh?'

'Guess she was kind of jealous. She trained that dog to go for me.'

'Pollution?'

'By name and by nature. It used to lie there growling so I couldn't write or read or think.'

Buck's heart lifted at the thought. 'Well,' he said to Gus, 'I'll see you around. Think I'd better start now.' He zipped and made rapidly for the door while Gus was in dejected mid-jet. Thank God he was not wearing a proper suit with buttons.

The poetry reading was not crowded, but not disgracefully empty. It took place in a room rather savagely adapted to its purpose, the kind of room where a revolutionary tribunal or an amateur jazz band might have met when traditional society had melted away into the streets. You could hear the snow-water of 1917 gurgling in the gutters of your mind, a melancholy sound. An official spoke in the warm, sensible voice of a primary-school teacher, but Buck was listening to the snow melting on cobblestones and melting onto snow. He was trudging forward through snow banks yellow with horse-piss and pink with raspberry-coloured blood. 'I know the force of words, the detonation of words.' He began to read.

He read in a daze, conscious only of his words and of the small crowd of hearers, a lady in a long dress smiling with pleasure like a Greek statue, an old destitute, bearded poet in training shoes, a sandy-haired man with bloodshot eyes, a dark-faced, sack-shaped publisher whose head drooped towards suicide. Two or three students. Loftus looking pleased. One part of Buck was coldly calculating, and the moment that he saw Loftus glancing at his watch he drew to a close, only three minutes over time. Applause came and went. Would he read one poem again? Would he read a little longer? He would. The applause was louder and longer the second time. It was final and dismissive. He signed some books. For a few minutes the evening seemed important and memorable, to him as well as them, but who would remember it in six weeks? Only Gus, who was conscious that Buck turned his back on him, and deliberately gave him the slip. You remember those you have injured more than those who injure you.

19d, Heath Lane,
Ealing

Dear Mike,

I have just bought your novel, like millions who read the reviews. I liked the first two very much, but this one really seems to be a breakthrough. Congratulations.

No news from Ealing, you will be unsurprised to hear. I have been attacked by premature male menopause. I am between girls, spouses, and so on, between styles and poems, and I dare say between prison sentences. Also between credit cards. It is very expensive being a successful ad man, you should have warned me.

The other day I gave a poetry reading, the first in years, impelled psychologically by old Loftus. I do not know whether he wanted it to succeed or (I suspected) fail, but did my best to please him both ways, and he seemed delighted at the end. Because it was over? Anyway, thank heavens Dizzy was not there. All that is over, and I only regret the dog.

I believe I will soon have to work for a health-food account and need to consult you. I will not eat the stuff but I see you describe it in this novel, and wondered whether we might film the little scene where they fall in love over the wholewheat flan. You are the only writer who can make it sound possible. Or have you already sold the film rights? I am serious about this.

Your poor old Buck

P.S. To the firm's fury I am having our offices very expensively redecorated with chintz walls. Come and see.

Yardstick and Cocker,
Soho Square

Dear Buck,

Thanks about the book. We have both reached a stage where success is just clocking up the opus numbers. It arrives when one no longer expects it, and seems as irrelevant as one always knew it would. Only those who achieve success, you more than me, retain their innocence, because without it we would overvalue it. But the money is nice.

I am going to host a new kind of TV arts programme all about the New Style, and I hope you will be one of the guests. No dons. No lefties. No fogies, new or old. We could film you with the chintz and that nice lady who makes your tea and opens your tins and bottles.

I am afraid I did sell the film rights, and you will have to deal with Curtis Brown. But I am sure a mutually agreeable deal could be arranged.

Will phone.

Mike

P.S. Am in New York for two weeks from Monday, for American publication of my novel.

When he got this letter, Buck was waiting for a Mozart concert on Radio 3, which he still thought of as the Third Programme '. . . a more mature work than the two we have just heard,' said the announcer, 'written when he was eighteen, and working as a court conductor in Salzburg.' Buck petulantly switched off, and continued with his word list. Yardstick. Haycock. Dog-eared. Dog violet. Dog-eared greenery of the dog violet. The rank smells of pollution in haycocks. The frizzled hayfield, haypath, path. The frizzled path beyond the kissing stile. It was a morning when he had endless insights into other people's poetry, but none into his own: a morning when stamina had become passive. His tea lady liked the chintz but thought it was a waste, and who was going to keep it clean?

He had a meeting planned for that morning with a lady from graphics. She had decided views and an iron constitution. They set out to sea on the good ship Bollinger at eleven in the morning; by three in the afternoon they had eaten nothing but olives and the time for lunch had somehow passed by. At four they were due at their printers, the last hot-metal printers in London, operated by elderly, non-unionized Poles whose uncertain grasp of English spelling and punctuation recalled the Elizabethan age. Buck was fond of these printers. He liked the impression of positive dents the print made on the paper. Liz, the graphics lady, disapproved of them. 'English is complicated enough,' she maintained, 'without it being altered by Polish exiles. Did you know the only reason we spell ghost with an aitch is because Caxton used foreign printers? Think of the culture shock.' Buck was entranced by this consideration. In fact, he began to fall under this lady's spell.

He asked her what she thought of his chintz. 'Pretty,' she said.

'Do you like it?'

'No.'

'Oh.'

'I see you're under the spell of Max Loftus.'

'Do you know him?'

'He's my uncle.'

'It's a small world.'

'It's a whirlpool, and he's in the middle of it.'

'He must be an interesting uncle.'

'Oh yes, as an uncle.'

Buck was not quite sure what to make of Liz. Any niece of Loftus was a formidable proposition to him.

Liz was a brisk and definite young woman, but not without compassion. 'Do you love it for the colours?' she asked him.

'We did have the London phone book, but that was a bit drab.'

'Oh. I'd have preferred that. Still, this must be a change from Dartmoor. It was Dartmoor, wasn't it?'

He found himself blushing, because no one in advertising usually referred to his prison adventure. He supposed Liz knew because Loftus must have told her. Having blushed, he began to smile.

'Dartmoor was a change from London,' he said, 'and this is a change from Dartmoor.'

Mrs Bates the tea lady popped in with some crab sandwiches, unordered, and a jug of orange juice.

Liz appraised her. 'She looks after you.'

'Yes, she's a change from Dartmoor as well.'

At no stage of their early acquaintance did Buck feel certain what Liz thought of him. The entry of Loftus into the relationship brought a dose of genetic interest, but no more light, since it was never clarity but only curiosity of many kinds that Loftus generated. Liz was her own woman, she attacked Buck contantly, always from unexpected angles, though attack is the wrong word as he soon saw. She prodded him with the persistent curiosity of a fish, but not a predatory fish. It was the certainty and what seemed to be the scientific basis of her views about graphics that puzzled him most of all. People from graphics in the agency where he worked were usually more docile. Liz knew the latest research on the dissolving focus of ageing eyes, she understood the effect of music on children in the womb, and of a more popular kind of music on the milk production of cows. Buck made a valuable suggestion about this. He suspected that the doctors who experiment on unborn babies like Purcell and Mozart, and people in milking sheds like romantic tunes, the qualities of the researcher affecting the research in both cases. Liz noted the possibility with a determined expression. 'Cows like what they see us like. Query babies.'

They survived their visit to the printers on the day Liz mentioned Dartmoor, but they were late, then the rush hour engulfed them. By the witching hour of half past six they were back in central London, in an underground bar with leather armchairs and bits of polished brass. Liz was explaining to Buck the effect of layout on the renaissance passion for sonnets which involved the need to close every sonnet sequence with a longer poem of another shape. Buck felt obscurely threatened by this information, and he inwardly resolved to pay more attention to the layout of his books. It looked for a sad moment as if he was going to buy a computer at last, but one grain of doubt survived: whether a computer could do his layout better than he might do it himself, and he nourished that grain. To him the layout of a poem was like a personal smell, a scent of intoxicating roses. He dared to say so to Liz, and she gave him an old-fashioned look. He was really quite drunk, she decided.

'My idea of cooking,' he said, 'is a page of poems gently simmered until you taste all the juices.'

'Men's cooking is drowning a mouse in gin.'

'A poem like a herbaceous border, full of little harvest mice asleep in their nest.'

'That's not the sort of poem you write.'

'It is when I'm drunk enough. Drinkwater. Vodka means water, so does whisky. I am the new Drinkwater.'

'What rubbish your head is full of.'

'My head is a teapot for vodka. It can hold one teapot filled up. If it fills up more than that I get drunk.'

'You are drunk.'

'Mmm. Maybe.'

Somehow she cast a spell over him. They were not immediate lovers but they became a couple, went everywhere together, entertained and got invited out together. Liz was an extension of Loftus's influence by other means. All the same Buck was taking on the air of a suffering clown, an ad man with his heart eaten out. His poetry was a seashore where the waves had withdrawn and the rock pools evaporated. He felt his earlier work had been heady with sexual disturbance, which his readers had greatly enjoyed without either writer or reader understanding what kind of disturbance was being communicated. Liz and Loftus had tampered in some dangerous way with his poetry. It had become more a matter of will, or of reason. He could write poems quite coldly now. Maybe every writer has to relive the literary history of their century. If that was true, he felt he had got to the year 1956, the triumph of The Movement and of Philip Larkin, the old lighthouse keeper of English literature. On the wall of his room in Ealing he kept photographs of poets he feared to become. He called them Know your Enemy. When he told Liz about this she made him take them down. In one way or another she calmed his fears of the future. Perhaps that was a mistake, but he felt it as a relief.

Her criticisms of his writing when she made any were

brief and clear. They tended towards normality, yet Liz was not at all a conventional woman. She could beat him at tennis or at chess, and everyone could beat him at snooker; he was nearly invincible only at poker. They liked to play it together, and in this at least she was pleased to submit to him. Loftus played poker too, it was among his accomplishments, and he could beat both of them. Once he took them out together in a motorboat in the Channel, not far from the shadow of the Isle of Wight, the white cliffs blazing and melting in pure sunlight. But Loftus showed little interest in the view or the weather. The purpose of the expedition was to play poker, and that is what they did, with little thought of the sea swell on which they floated. Buck remembered it later all the same, and it became for him an image of private friendship and tranquillity.

Buck and Liz went together to a party given by a television star they scarcely knew, in a London club that stood in a row of clubs looking out through enormous Victorian windows at some ordinary-looking yellow roses in the centre of an empty garden. The tallness of the rooms gave them the sad air of grandeur that the oldest European hotels used to have. London is full of such rooms, where life always seems to be over, and the receptions that have been held in them for a hundred and fifty years have left no lively dregs, no historic presences, only an absence, a sense that the party is over, an oppressive shrinking of expectations. Lancaster House, Buckingham Palace, the clubs in Pall Mall and so on, constitute one labyrinthine wilderness of rooms, where the same roar of voices ebbs and flows. Lord Longford, like an eccentric, paper-white moth, flits among the famous journalists and the laughing ambassadors. He smiles with sincere vagueness at Loftus, he beams with genuine curiosity at Buck. Liz is talking mustard to a cookery columnist. A minor royalty, small but real, has been cornered by David Frost. He is looking older, and at a party one is unable to switch him off.

The editor of the *Spectator* was chatting to an attentive priest on the edge of the stationary throng. Their ideas did not seem to be the same, though each in his own way was preposterously coherent, each had his personal brand of charm and sweet reason, but one may doubt whether either got past the other's defences. Yet their conversation was friendly and Mozartian. Loftus cast an avuncular beam at them both. Towards the centre of the room where he was headed, people were so crowded that only their mouths moved and their restless eyes. A publisher was exchanging Chinese courtesies with a successful professional lady whose name he had quite clearly forgotten. He must keep talking until he remembered it, so that he could bring it in and prove he knew it.

'So nice to run into you, Jenny darling, if running is the word.'

'Running may be the word but Jenny isn't the name. I'm Beatrice Miller.'

'Oh, of course. Yes, I knew. Beatrice. How silly of me.'

Liz had moved on to where she found herself among feminists being flattered by an actor, but there she soon got tired. She spotted Buck, far across the pillared room, staring at the books on the shelves. 'Oh, hullo,' he said when she got to him, 'I was thinking Henry James must have read these books.'

'I shouldn't think he'd do anything so ungentlemanly.

I'm sure they're not meant for reading.'

'Oh, I think they are. They look used and they don't match.'

'Did I hear you discussing the books?' A fattish, pinkish, bald-headed little man popped out from ambush. 'Indeed we do read them. A good historical library I always think.'

'Really?'

'Oh yes. Though of course some members come up here to sleep in the afternoons.'

'Oh. I see.'

'Mmm. Yeats used to read thrillers up here, not without a nap or two.'

'Did you know Yeats?'

'Oh yes. Dreary fellow. Very Irish. Do you happen to know who that girl is over there? I have an idea she's a Cavendish–Bentinck.'

'No, I don't know, I'm afraid.'

'No, quite. Awfully hard to tell them apart.' He buzzed off again like a small pink bumblebee; Buck never discovered who he was.

The slow, tidal movement of the party was beginning to empty the room. Here and there, people were writing names and numbers in small notebooks. Only the host was looking worn out with pleasure, wreathed around a pillar near the doorway. Loftus had gone off to dine somewhere, and the remaining stars were looking anxiously around their diminishing audience. One could distinguish separate sentences now from other people's conversations.

'That dress was Dior, I swear it.'

'My brother lives in Ireland. He knows a lot about it.'

'Who was that girl?'

'She's the one we met in the car park.'

'The Queen wasn't best pleased, I can tell you.'

'They're in Spain, aren't they?'

'No, they've just come back from Spain. They're in Venice.'

No one was drunk, no one was badly behaved, everyone was comparatively elegant. Buck and Liz enjoyed the absence of other advertisers, they enjoyed the adventure into a world not quite theirs, a world, as Buck reminded himself with a pang of fear, where they might easily have met the Haddalots. He wondered whether Loftus knew the Haddalots.

> 19d, Heath Lane,
> Ealing

Dear Liz,

What a noisy party. The upper class make a special noise and have a special combined smell against which the most individual French scent in the world, even your kind, cannot hold out. I think it is a flower called tuberose, and since people stopped smoking it has become overwhelming on what old Loftus calls a good scenting day. We must research this.

But I am really writing to say I have a cold in the head in Ealing, and when I get back to the office the rest of this week will be chaotic in consequence. Would have phoned you but assumed my cold to be a hangover but it is not. I am eating oranges and real old-fashioned aspirin. Hope you are well meanwhile. Let's plan for the weekend.

> Love, Buck

P.S. I am on the trail of a poem, but inspiration is mixed up with gluey cold or flu, and all lines that suggest themselves are short of breath. Resting between energetic sleeps last night I revalued much recent poetry and all other earths being stopped discovered this new style. Buck.

Between Islington and Ealing they trod a pathway. They knew many routes. In the brushed pine kitchen in Islington Liz planned his career. She sought through him for an ultimate urban morality, a poetry that might make sense for her of the inconclusive encounters, the disenchanted explorations of a life which in itself was radically incoherent. She was bright and definite all the same, and could never wholly suppress her good health and high spirits. After her most earnest, probing sentences, there would come a wild laugh and a flash of the eyes. In the unbrushed bedroom in Ealing, Buck distrusted general ideas and refused any ultimate form of morality, preferring as he told her the limited, diverse pleasures of suburban morals to all deep or pure considerations. He fingered his way through sheafs of general ideas as if they were rugs, for their texture but not really for their pattern. They were rugs he was not going to buy. His feeling for morality was a blind man's feeling for a rug. He invested his intellectual capital like Auden in the most expensive dictionaries, because he believed that poems were made of words. Another mistake.

Buck loved Loftus because Loftus had been an angler in the lake of darkness. He loved Liz because she stimulated him, every way but sexually, and probably at some level in that way as well. He was born to be cosy and domestic, though he had not achieved it and was unconscious of nature's purpose in him. She was an intellectual woman, proud of being professional and independent, intolerant of sexist men. They influenced each other, but Buck had moments of despair, in which he felt he should be returned to his maker for further instructions. The Vicar of Ealing lay in wait for him beyond some corner of his descending spiral, that luckily, perhaps because of Liz, he never passed. Liz had moments of blackness too, but Buck often found her unexpected solutions in verse or prose, and she brought him constant inspiration and a sense of light.

At times they quarrelled about this and that, but the underlying momentum of all the quarrels was to bring them closer. Once it was about politics and newspapers. Liz was meeting Buck at a café in Shepherd's Bush for breakfast, because they had to drive to some printers in Luton who produced posters in primary colours that looked like modernist prints. She was shocked to find him reading the *Morning Star*. If it had been *Marxism Today*, or even *Pravda*, she would not have minded, because that would have shown the exercise of a certain agility of mind. It would have been a serious game. But the *Morning Star* looked like an affectation. It looked like New York radical chic of the nineteen sixties. She could not bear to see him looking out of date.

'But I am out of date.'

'It's like a wrong note in music. Nobody admires you for it.'

'Poets are out of date. They are a wrong note in music. Nobody admires them but themselves.'

'Reading that rag doesn't make you poetic. It

impresses nobody. Serious communists read a proper paper.'

'So do I. I read all the papers. Today I have this one. I like it.'

'You don't like it, Buck, you only think you do.'

'You only pretend I don't because it embarrasses you.'

'Oh, don't be so silly. Grow up.'

And so on. It was early in the day, the traffic was bad, and no doubt they both had hangovers. They began to criticize one another's characters with passionate intimacy. Quarrels of that kind usually take place within families or among the young and immature. They have no good outcome except that a frustration expressed is diminished. But they can suddenly lead you to a critical moment, a parting of the ways that passes by before you realize that you could have chosen another direction. Buck and Liz were at least sufficiently mature to observe that moment when it loomed in sight, and to choose. They made love in a hotel in St Albans, rather as the young Graham Greene played Russian roulette on the gloomy common at Berkhamsted not far away, only in a more positive frame of mind. What began with deliberation and with an eye to consequences, like a move at chess, became gleeful, amusing, a relief.

'Buck?'

'Mmm?'

'Do you like my body? Do you?'

'Mmm.'

'Damn you, that's not much of an answer.'

'Of course I do. I always like people's bodies if I like them.'

'Sexist.'

'Yes.'

She gave him a leisurely scratch.

'Chauvinist pig.'

'Mmm.'

'What about men's bodies?'

'All bodies.'

'Liar.'

'You're my favourite.'

'Ever?'

'Ever.'

'Liar.'

'Mmm.'

Strange as it would have seemed to an earlier generation, and even to Loftus, who did observe a difference in them that week, neither of the new lovers believed that anything serious had altered in their relationship. They just felt they had avoided a disagreeable row, which in the last analysis was about sexual roles, by taking the obvious course of testing their roles by trial and error. It was a pleasing idea that they were lovers, but a thought without consequences. It was not meant to establish any permanent relationship, it was just a stage passed, like being on kissing terms in a society where not everyone kisses on sight. In Liz and Buck's world, almost everyone did kiss on sight, they also made love almost on sight. The provincial reader whom I most value will understand my need to explain all this.

19d, Heath Lane,
Ealing

Dear Mike,

I am thrilled you are such a success, and of course I will come to the party. Who would miss a ride in an airship? Or will it be moored at Croydon? You must think of us to manage your publicity. We are starting to run the personal publicity for writers instead of dealing just with publishers, who are too mean. You are at the stage when you could be marketed as yourself alone in two dozen languages.

My idea is that it would be quite easy to buy a small publishing house that a big group wanted to get rid of, and set it up again just for you. The bank's money, natch. We would set it up. All we need from you is normal disloyalty to your last publishers, whom I note have just been taken over anyway, for the second time in three years. In fact we might buy them, if you like the name, and if (as I am sure) the new owners have no real plans for them. Anyway I would like to talk about all this. You could be as big as Perrier water. We could introduce a lucrative side-line in mind-boggling fees for mentioning certain luxury brand names in your next. Don't sniff at this, because in your upper-class scenes your prose style would benefit by being more specific. People can't go on writing about James Bond's type of coffee for ever. Anyway it now costs too much for any normal hero to drink it. The food of heroes is bread and jam, as Joyce Cary remarked, and we have interesting butter and jam accounts. I admit no hero would eat the kind of bread we advertise. But you can choose.

You kindly ask about my Muse. She has nested in Ealing and become very suburban, but she is still laying eggs of an exquisite pale pink, and I won a prize for translated poetry in Hungary. I am supposed to be translating the Hungarian national poet in return, but I have forgotten his name and lost his book. Maybe we could visit him in your airship? I assume it's yours, as I cannot believe your publishers could afford to pay for it, even on your sales. Or is it a desperate attempt to impress the new owners? It won't. But I am looking forward to it very much indeed.

Buck

P.S. Do you mind if I bring Liz, as we are together at the moment?

The Connaught Hotel,
London W 1

Dear Buck,

Thanks for your letter. Must consult my tax accountant before answering it. If as I suppose all publicity and business expenses, including buying a publishing imprint, are tax allowable, your perspective is attractive. Otherwise I will have to end up living in the bloody airship over mid-Atlantic to escape the taxes on both sides. You're right about my owning it. See you on Sunday at Croydon. Don't be late as we shall leave moorings at 11 am come what may.

Mike

P.S. Sorry about Liz, but we shall be crammed to capacity that day. Any other weekend.

Buck explained this away to Liz as a business arrangement. Time being short, he chose to do so by telephone in working hours, a tactless decision as things turned out.

Brr—Brr. Brr—Brr.

'Yah?'

'Liz?'

'Yah.'

'Buck.'

'Yah.'

'Morning.'

'Morning.'

'You know Mike's airship party?'

'Yah.'

'It seems it's business only, and I'm not allowed to bring you. He says he's full up.'

'Are you still going?'

'Well, I have to for business reasons.'

'What reasons?'

'I have a scheme I want to put to him.'

'Damn him.'

'I suppose it's my fault really.'

'Damn you then.'

Click.

The airship loomed enormous over the old Croydon aerodrome, where Loftus kept his first private plane, and A.E. Housman used to take the air ferry for Paris in the days when that had only a windscreen and no closed cockpit.

'Larky for a don,' said Loftus.

'Not too larky for a Shropshire lad,' said Buck.

'Bromsgrove,' said Loftus. 'It's quite natural if you think of him as a poet from Bromsgrove. The motorway makes a difference of course, to the way one thinks about

Bromsgrove. Blue remembered hills on one side. Birmingham on the other.'

The airship's saloon car was pitifully small, and below it Croydon aerodome was just a handkerchief of grass. Far away in the haze a chain of dull gleaming patches of water indicated the lower Thames, winding from pool to pool. The saloon of the airship was overheated, and Buck regretted his stiff charcoal suit with the chalk stripes.

'What are you disguised as?' asked Mike.

'A success.'

'You're a famous poet, what more do you want?'

'Money. Works of art on the wall. Airships.'

'Do you like her, really?'

'Mmm. She's a bold gesture.'

'Come and meet David. You'll like him.'

'Who's David?'

David was dancing on his own to the music of what looked like a computer, though its voice was one of those infinitely refined versions of rock music that play ingeniously the role of immediate passions that time has swallowed. What did they feel like forty years ago? David's silk shirt was open to the navel. He was smooth and tan-coloured and expensive and would not last long, but Mike obviously adored him. As a way of showing David off and keeping things discreet at the same time, the airship was a sort of solution. Buck could understand that. And a party in an airship must have a defined ending, a terminus. Loftus was viewing David with mild disfavour. There was an observation deck outside in the wind swept by loud silence.

David had intense eyes that symbolized a hungry curiosity for life, or at least for everything in the world that he still innocently desired. He was still so young that every new character in his saga seemed to him to hold the key to a revelation. He thought them extraordinary. He did not understand himself to be ordinary or his charm to be brief or his innocence to be ignorant. He would end up running an antique shop in Kensington Church Street. He would button up his shirt.

To David, Buck had the incandescent charm of experience, not just as a druggy but as a poet and a man of business. No one but David really admired Buck's brand new pin-stripe suit. In turn, no one but Buck admired David's provincial quality, which under the skin they both shared. Mike had never really noticed it in either of them, being an idealist. It was not observation that had drawn him to fiction, but the desperate need to express something. The something had an all but erotic immediacy, which was why his novels were now selling millions of copies. It was the force that through the green fuse drives the flower, which no one can define but everyone can recognize.

Mike had no time at his own party for a private conversation with his poet. To tell the truth, he was still a little in awe of Buck, as he always had been. He was prepared to stand up for prose against poetry, but secretly he knew himself to be a failed poet, and believed Buck must be a poet born not made, because his own attempts at poetry had rung hollow. Buck had admired them all the same, and that had been the first basis of their friendship. Now Mike was so successful that socially at least he could relax. On his airship he was the boss, the host and the patron. He was glad to see young Buck and young David get on well together. It would be good for clever David to know brilliant Buck, that was why he had asked him. He was not in the least jealous, of course he was not.

Buck and David exchanged a gesture of wanting to see one another again, the tentative first sketch of an arrangement. That might have come to nothing, but Mike made an excuse of his business dealings. They might come back to his place in the afternoon, but he had to have lunch with his lawyer before he could talk to Buck. When could Buck offer him something on paper? If he could have it by Wednesday, then why should he not try it out on his lawyer on the Monday? It could all be fitted in before Mike took David to New York? They had tickets for a ballet there. 'And it's the only place,' said Mike, 'to buy my kind of pictures.'

Whether or not because this raised the movement of money and the exercise of patronage, the remark attracted several people's attention. It injected the moment with a coarse elecricity. Names flared and faded.

'Betty Boop.'

'Mary Cassatt.'

'Rothko?'

'Things have moved on since Rothko.'

'New York's about the only place things do move on.'

'They move backwards in London.'

'Move?' interjected Loftus. 'They have a stagnant circularity, they don't move at all. Modern art is over, and from my old-fashioned viewpoint that's a great relief.'

Buck turned to him. 'I thought you enjoyed it,' he said. 'It was your generation.'

'Oh no,' remarked Loftus with a sage expression,

'speed without movement, that was my ideal.'

The others made what they could of this remark, but no one was bold enough to contradict him.

'Like dancing,' said David.

'Nothing to do with art,' said Loftus. 'Nothing to do with modern art.'

So Buck and David met for lunch in a small, almost modish restaurant, too newly opened to be crowded at lunch time. It was full of light, having a huge plate-glass window that framed a view of dustbins and drainpipes, and snowy white interior walls achieved with numerous coats of whitewash. The furniture was straw-coloured and the food was light-hearted. Nothing much happened at lunch except that they liked each other more rather than less. They became quite painlessly a little drunker than they realized on a giant-sized carafe of Californian white wine, but the coffee was plentiful and very strong. The trouble was that Buck had felt slightly awkward about telling Liz he was meeting David, as he had done about describing the airship party. Liz with mild but gleeful malice was sitting at another table. She knew all about what went on in the airship from Loftus. How was she to know how prejudiced his account had been? She smiled a steely smile, and she waved; she ate with an old beau now silver-haired; if she had time she would have organized a large and noisy party to draw David's attention. As it was she left the restaurant before they did.

'Who was your friend?'

'Oh he's a friend of Mike's. I told you about him.'

'Saving his soul, are you?'

'Not at all. Who were you with?'

'Henri. He's a decorator. I must say he was rather interested in your friend.'

'Mike's friend.'

'Your friend's friend. He thought you had him nicely placed to match the Hockney on the wall.'

'I didn't see the Hockney on the wall.'

'You had no eyes for anything, did you? Low score for a poet.'

'I was entertaining somebody.'

'Why don't you write a poem about him? Then you can put the lunch down to expenses.'

That was the end of that conversation. The final remarks gave full expression to a momentary anger which alarmed them both, because it seemed to have taken over Liz, altered her character, and left her terribly vulnerable. As a remark it rankled only slightly and briefly. Buck was used to heavier and more searching insults: he was well used to people saying 'write a poem about it'. When he next made love to Liz, which happened within hours, she was more passionate than before, and so was he. She bit him and he sweated a strange, sweet-smelling sweat. *Ulularunt vertice nymphae.* Loftus howled on the crest of the mountain.

19d, Heath Lane
Ealing

Dear Loftus,

I saw Mike the other day, back from New York and more confident than ever. They are pressing him to sign a contract for his next three books over there. They would publish them in England through a publisher they already own. I have got him to delay a week, and now is the time to activate my scheme, which I told you about on the day of the airship. Can I rely on your support to do this under cover of the agency, that is within the agency?

I would have liked to see you to discuss this at the weekend, but I had to go fishing with Mike and David as they have bought several miles of Scottish river and none of their other friends like fishing unless you do. I have only fished for sea bass before, in the Bristol Channel, so this was an opportunity.

Buck

P.S. I think fishing poetry might be my new subject. Unfortunately, there is a surprising amount of it already, but at least I could anthologize it. Do you know a publisher anxious to earn some prestige and lose some money?

Loftus & Loftus
Aeronautical Engineers

Dear Buck,

No sound publisher wants to earn prestige, nor can it be earned by losing money. Have you not learnt that?

As for Mike's arrangements, I do not think you should interfere. Should you decide to do so, then it must be outside the agency and without cover from me. The factor that determines his great and astonishing attraction as an investment is, of course, his film, television and video rights. If you had done your homework you would have discovered that the agency is heavily committed to R P J International, who control the exercise of those rights. To break that commitment would lead to cash flow difficulties for several subsidiaries, and would be a dangerous move to make. My advice is, stick to poetry.

Yours,

Loftus

P.S. I hope that young man is better at fishing than he is at dancing. In any event I think you ought to stop teasing Liz.

Mythology always points to a crisis in the early career of the successful tycoon: the cornering of a monopoly, the invention of a market, the birth of the first million. The truth is that real tycoons have a crisis every week, sometimes three a day; in all of them their touch is faultlessly golden. For those who fail to become tycoons every crisis that does come along leads to a new failure. They are always resitting the same elementary examination in economics. Life sets it before them again and again from various different directions, but they will never understand. Buck was like that. Something might still have been made of his idea, because no formidable forces were against him except the law of probabilities. Yet he did too little as well as too much. He alienated Loftus his mentor, he annoyed him seriously, because Loftus had schemes and angles of his own. Buck found himself in trouble with his parent company. He made a feint of persisting, he lost himself in a labyrinth of negotiations about money which had a geometric beauty but no reality. Suddenly he was dropped, isolated, sacked, in the street, nearly on the dole. At this stage he dropped his scheme and admitted his despair. He did so both too early and too late. No one appeared to have any intention of rescuing him. In matters like these it was obvious to them all that Buck was born to be a failure.

His financial collapse was not quite complete all the same. Liz first and then other old colleagues found him freelance work that they knew he could do well. Mike assured him that if he found partners he could still be set up in an agency of his own. But he found no partners, and Mike was too busy to talk business. He was off to Paris to launch David in French television, off to Hollywood to launch him in films, off to a private Greek island to launch him socially. David opened his amazing eyes very wide, and smiled in a bemused manner. Buck depended mostly on Liz. She was faithful by temperament and she enjoyed scolding him, two useful ingredients for a girl in her position. The removal of David from Buck's sphere must also have reassured her, though she kept a cold eye on him afterwards. Her opinions were liberal: yet it was more the idea of David than his reality that had shaken her. She had of course imbibed that idea from old Loftus.

But as consequence followed consequence and the next stage of Buck's destiny unfolded, Loftus was won round by him. Buck in despair became hectic. He tried to market a scent called hay and roses, and mounted an advertising campaign to raise money for some nuns which came close to bankrupting them. The nuns were a turning point; he became interested in the titles of the curious pamphlets they sold to their supporters. He made jokes about these pamphlets, and in the end one joke too many. The rumour crackled around London that Buck was writing a pamphlet called 'Jesus and the meaning of shopping'. A gossip column reported it, a reporter followed it up, Buck was interviewed, publishers approached him. The momentum of this idea carried him beyond fantasy to a point where he had to sit down and write. The result brightened a dull issue of *The Sunday Times*, for several weeks it was famous, a Marxist bishop called it Mrs Thatcher's gospel, lesser comedians made jokes about it; as a paperback it sold more copies than any other book that Buck ever wrote. Loftus was amused. Liz was pleased. Smile and the world smiles with you, thought Buck.

Escapade after escapade does not amount to a career all the same. His poetry suffered from neglect and from the absorption in life of the energies that had nourished it. The heart had gone out of his work, then it went out of his business life, and out of his bizarre relationship with Loftus, because Loftus smiled too knowingly, and out of his affair with Liz, because he cooled as she became more passionate. He was tired out. He was tired of advertising, of bad taste, of easy money, of ugly London. He was tired of himself. Old weariness and buried anxieties rose from their graves to haunt him. His image in the shaving mirror tormented him, the desire Liz felt for him was no longer a comfort, it no longer made him think well of himself. At some deep level he was frightened. He was like an old soldier whose nerve has suddenly failed.

The break with Liz did not come easily. He had taken again to haunting the Museum of Mankind, and Sir John Soane's Museum where his favourite thing was a collection of ancient Greek temples carved out of cork. One day he came on a young girl in a sort of conservatory there, intently recording a queer jumble of Hellenistic marble fragments, but when he passed behind her he saw that the drawing in her sketchbook was completely abstract. He laughed to himself. Then the next week he saw the same girl in the Museum of Mankind, recording the apparatus of a Mexican undertaker's shop with just the same passion. She was a pretty creature with tight curls and pink cheeks, obviously an art student. He could not resist talking to her. She seemed to like him, her voice was charming, she had a fresh Pennine accent and the Royal College was her idea of heaven. She was very young. They began to meet nearly every day. Liz suspected nothing, and Buck had no idea whether to tell her. He was not shocked by his own faithlessness, he just noted with interest that it had become natural to him to betray. Things had not always been like that, or he supposed not. Maybe we get coarser and worse all our lives, he thought, until we luckily die.

She was called Judy and he found her irresistible. She was as serious about her art and as old-fashioned in her principles about it as a Jewish refugee of eighty, but she was a hero-worshipper of people, including Buck. She knew his poems and blushed at his name. She was completely uninhibited by conventional morality, being the daughter of a high-minded pair of schoolteachers who reared her on D. H. Lawrence and the works of Darwin. She was collecting abstract watercolour drawings to illustrate *The Voyage of the Beagle*. She made two portraits of Buck for it, one as a series of grey triangles modulating into a background of white hoops, and the other as blue and yellow blotches with an autumnal air. They made love happily and often. Liz guessed of course.

Yet it was difficult for Buck to confess the truth to Liz.

74

He was not a believer in the virtue or the usefulness of truth-telling except in small, practical doses. Liz on her part was reluctant to bring the subject up. She sensed that this was a far more serious division between them than David could ever have represented. She felt dreadfully insecure. But as the affair drifted on it became a whirlpool, and the moment of drowning arrived. Buck and Liz were in the suburbs together on advertising business, in search of a man who made lithographs, painting his colours straight onto the stone. The lithographer worked in an old coal office in a railway siding, which was approached from the road by way of a shopping precinct where nasturtiums flourished in concrete tubs.

'I have to tell you, Liz, something I expect you guessed.'

'Tell me then.'

'It's another girl.'

'Yes.'

'It doesn't mean anything. It's not the same as you. It's just I find her irresistible.'

'Who is she?'

'A painter. You met her once.'

'Judy?'

'Did you guess?'

'No. No, I didn't. She's so young and such a lousy painter.'

'You and me matter in a different way.'

'Damn you. What *can* you mean?'

'Hearts apart but not asunder.'

'Damn you. Damn you. Damn you. I hate you and I despise you. I don't ever want to see you again. Not at

75

work. Not anywhere. Just get out of my life.'

'But Liz.'

'Get out, I said. Go. Get out.'

She began to shout, and people turned their heads to stare. She was pale with fury. As he walked away from her, he found himself weeping. This was not at all the scene that he intended. He wanted a conversation between musical instruments, he wanted the subtle correspondence of linked verses in Japanese poetry, perhaps he understood nothing at all about other people, nothing that was not poetry. He told himself so, but it was no comfort. He sat a long time over cups of coffee in the deadliest, gloomiest café he could find. It was not his failure to be faithful to Liz that worried him, but the failure of that last, awful conversation. She had been more hurt than he thought possible. She must have taken their affair so much more deeply than he supposed. As he sat over his puddle of muddy coffee he gazed blankly at a juke-box, scarcely aware when it was silent or when it played. He came to some resolutions. As for Liz, had he but known it she was furiously offended rather than deeply hurt. He took her weeks, not years, to get over.

But he decided on that afternoon to give up advertising, to give up London, to give up his way of life. At least she could never accuse him of just leading the same kind of life with a different partner. He would show her the change was a wrench if she threw him out. The change was going to be serious. He was going to become a serious person.

One may doubt whether he had chosen in Judy the ideal companion, or a possible companion at all, for such a change of life. But when he took so warmly to Judy, Buck had not intended or foreseen any far-reaching changes. He was just a duck taking to water. However, things fell out strangely as they sometimes do. Judy was tired of being a student: she wanted to get out of London and try the effect of what she called a heavy affair. Those were the days when people of her generation were terrified by AIDS. Two of her friends had taken to heroin, one had died by suicide. She felt the cold air as death passed close to her for the first time. She wanted to paint on her own, in the country, she wanted Buck to live with her away from crowds and concentrate on his wonderful poems, in which she had more faith than he had at that time.

Even so, they lacked an economic or a physical basis for their flight into the wilderness. It was hard to see who was going to help them. But death had been busy elsewhere. Only a day or two after he parted from Liz and fixed on his new life, Buck ran into Hamsyn Haddalot, now twenty years old. 'How's the cricket then?' Hamsyn blushed and giggled. He was a tall, cheerful young man, with an air of confident idiocy.

'How's Dizzy?' he answered without malice. 'Do you see her still?'

'No, not really, do you?'

'No, she's cut us off. She's in America I think. Dad left her lots of dollars.'

'Left her? Did your father die?'

'Oh yes, didn't you know? And mum. In my last year at school.'

'I'm sorry.'

'Never mind.'

'So what are you doing?'

'Oh, I'm stinking rich. I inherited. I have houses and factories and stuff. I sold Fingest and some of Dad's ugliest pictures, and bought another estate with a nicer house and twenty cottages. I own the village.'

'Good heavens.'

'You don't want to be vicar, do you?'

'No, but I wouldn't mind a cottage. In fact I'm desperate for one.'

'What, seriously?'

'Yes.'

'Well come down at the weekend. I own the cricket team as well as the village. Will you play?'

'Of course.'

'Alone or – er – ?'

'With a girl called Judy. She paints.'

'Oh good, can she do frescoes?'

PART THREE

'The sycamores are hissing,' said Buck. 'Whispering. Whooshing. Not soughing. What do sycamores do in the rain?'

'Shush,' Judy answered. 'They don't do anything. They just stand there like cows.'

'Sycamores look like leather and cows look like silk.'

'Maybe.'

They got on with their work with the door open between their rooms. Buck was writing a landscape book in an outworn manner to go with some photographs. Judy's paintings were getting bigger, she was winding herself up for the fresco.

Brr—Brr. Brr—Brr.

'Damn.'

'You answer it. I've got paint on my hands.'

'Buck? That you?'

'Hamsyn?'

'Yah. You two free for lunch tomorrow?'

'Oh, er, well, er, Yah. Yah, thanks.'

'Good. We might have some nets afterwards.'

'Er, yah. Yah.'

'Do you like dried seaweed?'

'Mmm, er . . .'

'Or whitebait?'

'Whitebait?'

'Tiny herring. They should be able to get us some. You have to wait for a frost.'

'Lovely.'

'Right. Quarter to one for drinks.'

Buck and Judy's cottage was not a thing of great beauty, though it had a curiosity value. It was an ornamental building with a thatched roof and Gothic windows, dating from those expansive days when gentlemen employed a peasant to impersonate a hermit in his cave, and had the scything of their grass done by moonlight to preserve their solitude dawn to dusk. The cottage was coloured deep pink like a strawberry mousse, sitting on an artificial lettuce leaf of cropped grass. Through the railings of its little garden, the Fingest goats craned their necks to loot its flowers and nose at its dustbins. Buck secretly liked it better than any house he had ever lived in. It was not as leafy as Ealing, but simpler, and he liked the seaside.

Hamsyn's house was tall and plain and very handsome. Grass lapped its walls, fallow deer in pretty groups wandered through the park. The goats had a smaller park of their own. Beyond the furthest trees lay the expiring sea. It was a famous view. The land was in the hands of agents and farmers and foresters. Sea-fishing and river-fishing and culling of the herd and gathering of gulls' eggs and plovers' eggs, the old sheep from the hillside and the young lambs from the salt marsh, all contributed to the income and the hospitality of the great house. Cricket was played all summer, every weekend and many evenings. The place was an attractive investment; the accountants were delighted with Hamsyn.

Judy liked the plainness of Hamsyn's house outside and in, she relished the peculiar texture of its bricks, she observed the stringent revelations that took place when the wind stripped away the clouds from the blue sky and light streamed everyhere. She looked forward to winter stripping away the heavy greenery from the trees in just the same way. Already she noted promising yellow leaves on the horse chestnuts near Gothic Cottage. The yellow leaves suited the black and white goats. She was painting a fresco round the real tennis court that Hamsyn had installed in an eighteenth-century barn to burn off some of his abundant energies. The fresco began as an abstract frieze but the goats broke through. They were geometric skeletons of goats in severe black and whites, they were by no means pastoral, in fact they were threatening, but they were real. Hamsyn had converted Judy from abstraction, which was more than the Royal College had been able to do, and more than Buck had presumed to attempt.

The barn still smelt faintly dank and sweet, as if the smells of two hundred years of harvest had stained it for ever. When they first came down there, Hamsyn had challenged Buck to a game of real tennis. Buck had incautiously agreed, but he was defeated, exhausted and humiliated. His limbs ached for days at the colossal attempt. The only consoling feature of the awful occasion was that Hamsyn was a good-tempered winner. He was, as he said, used to winning ball-games; he never minded the quality of his opponents, he just liked to play. All the same, Buck was unnerved. He never played real tennis again, though he liked to watch it, taking an ironic pleasure in the uninterrupted series of Hamsyn's victories. What he liked about the barn was its residual atmosphere of barn. Judy's fresco amazed him too. Every day it seemed to bring out new powers in her.

The stronger she became, the more he hated the book he was writing. He had a little money put by, but his work ethic as a writer drove him hard. He would not have dared fail to finish his book. Maybe all this was a way of avoiding the poems that were waiting to be written, because unwritten poems cry out for personal change.

They almost never went to London, though Hamsyn went. As time went by they wrote little to their friends, and after the first quarterly bill they telephoned much less. Very occasionally friends of Judy's would arrive in a second-hand motor car or by taxi from the station, but these interruptions meant little. They saw Hamsyn, and Hamsyn's friends. Buck was relieved that the cricket season was soon over. Hamsyn kept a horse or two for riding, but he was not on good terms with the local hunt. He often went out shooting, and sometimes fishing, but in these sports Buck was not expected to join. Hamsyn had placidly accepted that Buck was a duffer. He liked Buck very much indeed, but only for conversation in the evenings. He saw more of Judy, because when she painted in the barn he often came by.

Sometimes they met at formal dinners. These were spirited entertainments, neither as dull nor as grand as they may sound. The food was usually fresh and appetizing, and the drink delicious, though it was sometimes bizarre. One long evening they drank nothing but vodka, on another they finished most of a case of very old and urinous champagne. The guests varied equally. Sometimes Hamsyn brought down girlfriends, large, hearty girls whom he treated with sisterly affection. They were expensively dressed and good sports, but there was little else to distinguish one from another. Their mothers had known Hamsyn's mother or their brothers had been to school with him. It was the older guests who were peculiar. Buck found himself pinned to a corner of the drawing room by an oldish, baldish man, bright-eyed and dim-witted, who wanted to give the Elgin Marbles back to Turkey for a museum of Turkish Imperial History in Istanbul. At dinner an old Anglo–Irish lady explained how you could tell the condition of deer by their fewmets. He was pleased with the word fewmets. He thought of them as the central metaphor of a sonnet, or of one of those sarcastic, neoclassic poems that Eliot wrote on holiday in Henley or was it Marlow in the twenties.

At the far end of the table Judy was getting on well with a lugubrious art critic. He was like an old and melancholy lizard, gazing at her with considering eyes. Buck felt a bit jealous of the art critic. On his other side he had a very old lady indeed, the art critic's mother, who was getting on famously with one of Hamsyn's hearty young women, while Hamsyn sat between them, cheerfully bemused after an epic game of golf. Buck caught the eye of the man opposite him, who seemed to be a cousin, apparently a lawyer of some kind. He sat oddly upright and his eyes were cold, but he put away more Californian burgundy than anybody. Buck engaged him in a guarded conversation about last Sunday's book reviews. The cousin read the *Sunday Telegraph*, the *Spectator* and *The Times*. He sternly disapproved of the *Independent*. He preferred biography to fiction. Buck disengaged and returned to the diseases of deer and the different diseases of sheep. 'Where I come from in Ireland,' said the lady, 'people are so poor that no one can afford to keep their deer-parks in repair, and the deer are getting out everywhere.'

'Goats are worse,' said Buck, 'if they ever got out.'

They sat over dinner a long time. Later they all trooped across to see Judy's fresco. One large goat on a crag, the master-goat or protogoat of the painting, was finished in gleaming black and cream. The analysis of his shape was very like that of the rock, so that if he had been painted grey it would have been hard to pick him out of his background. All over the fresco other goats stood half-finished, alone or in groups, among unfinished rocky landscape. Some were hardly sketched, they might have been the scattered pieces of dismantled bicycles.

It was on these that the art critic lavished his praises. At the mastergoat he only smiled politely and said: 'Ghika? Picasso? Mmm?' Judy looked as if she could have hit him. A tiny tear trickled. Hamsyn swiftly hugged her. 'I think they're *wonderful*,' he said. 'I'm very pleased.' The Irish lady peered at the pure rocks for traces of fewmets. Buck talked sternly to the art critic about colour and form. 'What,' he asked, 'would a colourless form be like?'

'The soul,' replied the art critic.

Hamsyn gave Judy another hug, and she cheered up. She helped him explain the relevance of the fresco to real life and revolution to the art critic's mother. The sporting girl wandered up and down the fresco calling out, 'God I like this', and 'God this is good' to no one in particular. The legal cousin sneered silently.

Buck hardly noticed what was beginning to happen between Hamsyn and Judy. Indeed, their increasing and instinctive closeness had not yet passed any critical point. They had not so much a relationship as a continuous warmth, with sudden moments of affection forgotten as swiftly and as serenely as they arose. The next day for example, Buck had to go to London to take his finished book to the expectant publisher. Judy worked all morning at her sketches, then had lunch and a game of snooker with Hamsyn and the hearty girl, who was extremely nice to her. In the afternoon she walked to the village, where she bought a pot of dahlias and a bag of buns for Buck, to please him when he got home. He really was pleased too. So was she, because he bought her a silk scarf from London, and the *Burlington Magazine*. After supper he read her Browning while she set to work on the glossy illustrations.

Buck's scruffy and watch-chain-dangling Oxford tutor had been a Browning enthusiast, so the poems were familiar territory. Judy liked poetry indiscriminately, but what she really liked was Buck's voice reading it, which made Eliot sound like Browning and Rupert Brooke like Tennyson. His voice was iron in a velvet glove, not as subtle as you thought at first, but Judy felt his voice was one of the best things about him. She also felt he had particularly long legs and a big forehead, which poets ought to have. She saw the skull beneath the skin. She had a goat's skull in her studio, and would have liked a human skull as Browning had. He was reading her 'Piano di Sorrento', from *The Englishman in Italy*. She luxuriated in the luscious textures, without any expectation of strong shapes, so as the poem developed it surprised her, rather as her own painting surprised her more than it surprised other people. ' . . . the flat sea-pine crouches, The wild fruit-trees bend, E'en the myrtle-leaves curl, shrink and shut: All is silent and grave: 'Tis a sensual and timorous beauty. . . .' But then the sun comes out, and the secret of life dissolves.

All round the glad church lie old bottles
   With gunpowder stopped,

Which will be, when the Image re-enters,
　　Religiously popped;
And at night from the crest of Calvano
　　Great bonfires will hang,
On the plain will the trumpets join chorus,
　　And more poppers bang . . .

'Lovely,' she sighed at the end. 'You could almost paint it.'

'Not me. It's a conjuring trick really, not a world. Like the scorpion jumping out of the wall. He makes it all so foreign.'

'Glamorous and simple.'

'My fresco's not glamorous, but it is complicated.'

'I know.'

They murmured on and on for hours like that.

'You're Mr Burblethwaite and I'm Mrs Cowmire,' said Judy. 'We have pews on opposite sides of the church. We aren't the same.'

Buck did more burbling, but that was because he was less committed to the deeper levels of the conversation. At his most serious, he was laconic. For Judy words were a relaxation, a game she enjoyed playing. She did more trudging and squelching as she talked than Buck, she was a slower mover and grazer, but her footprints sank deeper into the ground. She thought the fact, if it was one, that things had to seem foreign to Browning before he could cope with them in poetry, was a flaw in his achievement and a grave fault in his art. That no doubt was her parents' high-mindedness coming out in her. Buck would sacrifice anything and adopt every strategy, sometimes two at once, in order to make a poem. He had

little notion of integrity and no distaste for the glamorous
or the exotic, if he thought he could get away with it. His
mind was just settling on the theme for what he foresaw
as a major poem, an elegy for the early Auden, an ode to
Auden and Isherwood on their departure for the United
States in 1939. The difficulties of this project gave him an
occasion for exaltation and for glorying in his powers
which he seldom enjoyed nowadays. He crossed and
recrossed his long legs. He reckoned he was ripe for
success.

Next day turned to sharp sunshine with a sting in it.
The grass was blazing green. Hamsyn's house had a pale
glitter, but the barn looked like a gem of architecture, as
perhaps it was. The apples were ripening. Buck walked
up to the tennis-court fresco with Judy, but he left her at
the door, to stride away on his own across the park,
planning his poem. He had a bit of paper for scribbling his
notes as the lines fell into place. He smelt a difficulty in
the idea of America. Auden he thought was setting out
for an idea, but America is not just an idea. Still, he could
make something of the machinery, the America of
Whitman, the New York of Lorca. He should have seen
that this was not going to be a great or even a good poem,
but he was too deeply immersed in its problems and
possibilities to notice what was wrong. He would have
done better maybe to write about the apples ripening
around him, but then he would have been a different
kind of poet. His poetry was, as we saw, an attempt to
become different, but the journey was a long one, the
process was a lifework.

He should have spent more of the day with Judy. While
she laboured so intently over her sketch-books at Gothic

Cottage, and he groaned over his landscape book in the next room, things were fine between them. But at the moment he was wrapped up in his poetry, and while Judy worked alone at the real tennis court Hamsyn often dropped in. He began to see more of her than he did of Buck. She liked Hamsyn a lot. He was so at home in his skin, so innocently cheerful. One day he came home from London with cocaine. He found her dejected, glowering at her second and third goats, longing for company and missing Buck.

'The goats ought to be more like the rocks,' she said. 'Or the rocks ought to be more like the goats.'

'Do you think cocaine would help?'

She tried it.

Hamsyn was quite open about this, but he happened not to see Buck for the next three or four days. His life was far busier than theirs. He left Judy a little supply of white powder to keep with her paints and brushes and rags in the barn, to use it when she needed. She was shy of telling Buck, she would have shared it with him but she imagined his disapproval, and after all it was Hamsyn's secret. It was an expensive, secret present, that separated Judy from Buck more fatally than just tumbling into bed with Hamsyn would have done. But that followed, as an impartial observer had there been one would have agreed that it must do. It was Hamsyn in the end who told Buck about the cocaine, diffidently suggesting it might do as much good for poetry as it did for painting. Buck said his senses were sufficiently disorientated and as for his wits, he needed them as they were. Hamsyn thought Buck cold and a little ungrateful, but he shrugged his shoulders and grinned at Judy.

Soon they talked about their entanglement, all three together, in the hope that it was not too late to do so. Hamsyn hung his head a little and said that he loved Buck almost more than Judy. He always had loved Buck. He said he could never have loved Judy without loving Buck first. He could never love anyone, any girl, except like that.

'You mean I'm a sort of donkey-engine?' asked Buck.

'More or less. But I still do love you.'

Judy was gazing from one to another, open-eyed.

'I love you both,' she wailed. 'I love you both more and more. But I don't like this donkey-engine idea.'

'It's how you're made,' said Buck. 'It's how things happen to be.' He wondered if he ought to slide one arm round each of them, but he found that impossible. Only Judy really had the right to love them both, so he supposed. Fortunately she did so.

'Why don't we live all three together?' she asked with a shade too much enthusiasm.

'Why don't we?' asked Hamsyn, in a relieved voice.

Something in Buck that felt like wounded pride was reluctant to accept this arrangement. At the same time he was sure that any conscious decision of his own would at the best be folly, a perilous intrusion on their fragile human affections, and one that might have unknowable consequences. His wisdom extended no further. He was willing to learn, willing to try anything once. Or was the truth that he belonged among those who by failing to understand their own sins and mistakes are perpetually doomed to repeat them? This thought undoubtedly occurred to him, but he knew that he was not on top of things. He just played along. He reckoned he was not physically in love with Hamsyn, but if asked he would have answered that in that kind of area of Eros, who knows? How much better off are those who know? He played along with the others. He became their analyst, their joker, and their magician. He made them all seem to themselves supremely funny, supremely blessed, uniquely and delightfully intertwined. His talk was intoxicating, they lived enchanted evenings and weeks. Yet this was not the bread and butter of life. Maybe the tragedies that overcome us are unreal. Maybe they are things of the mind that we nourish and breed up to devour us. If we choose we might be rid of them, Buck believed. But what overcame him was not precisely a tragedy, only a piece of everyday reality. Judy became pregnant by Hamsyn. They were both extremely pleased. Hamsyn warbled wildly about marriage. He wanted a little boy, though Judy knew from the beginning she was going to have a little girl. They were married just before Christmas: Judy moved into the big house, but she also kept her toehold in Buck's cottage.

Buck found himself a voyeur whether he liked it or not. On the whole he liked it. Hamsyn put off the honeymoon until February, to escape the worst English weather, the sea-fog and the gales and the driving rain. Buck was distinctly disappointed not to be asked, but he had experience enough of three-cornered honeymoons to see that it was unwise to press the point. In all other matters, Hamsyn was sunny and generous, and apparently more in love with Buck than ever. Judy was happy too, though she sometimes looked or sounded puzzled. Hamsyn kept up little of the routine of a great house. He had daytime help from the village, but no servant living in. When his friends came down from London it was only to play cricket or to shoot. Someone often brought cocaine. They wandered through the old rooms like barbarian aristocracy through the pleasure-houses of the Roman bourgeoisie, like young milords through the great houses of France after Waterloo. Buck avoided them. Hamsyn and Judy and Buck all slept with one another, sometimes all three together. All the same, Buck suspected that when friends came from London they took new partners.

Hamsyn and Judy were sure they were going to have a little girl; they were going to call her Jasmine. If it was a boy he could be called Tocsin; the names were Judy's idea. Buck thought them ridiculous, and said so.

'What about you being called Buck? That's pretty far out for a vicar's son?' He blushed. He was unable to admit it stood for Buckingham, where he was conceived. Still, he persisted that a boy called Tocsin would be bullied at school.

'Not at Eton,' said Hamsyn. 'Till then he could have a tutor. I wondered if you might tutor him?'

Buck got out of this by claiming his Latin was rusty. The thrilling day came when Judy gave birth to twins.

'Well then,' said Hamsyn, 'they can sit in a hedge and teach each other. They must never, never be separated.'

It was at this time that Buck felt really out of things. Everyone still loved him, but during Judy's pregnancy his affair with her ended. He was short of money too, and his ode to Auden was a failure. In the end he transformed it into a life of Auden in verse like John Betjeman's *Summoned by Bells*. Following the same example, he sold his poem to the *New Yorker*. That was what drew him into writing for magazines as a new career.

Bits of his poem were rather good, particularly the English scenery, the smooth green hills, the quarries scooped in the rocks, and the sea-sand as brown as an egg. But the whole poem was not what Judy expected of him. After the birth she went through severe depression. The twins were tiring, but she insisted on doing everything for them herself; even Hamsyn was scarcely allowed to help. The strain increased the depression; cocaine was her only comfort. When she went back to work at last for just an hour or two a day she worked with a grim intensity. On the day that Buck finally left for New York, Hamsyn found her working on a self-portrait in the fragments of a broken mirror, while her indestructible twin babies played among her paints.

Hamsyn did what he could for her, but he had little idea what to do. They both hated doctors. They believed only in decoctions of honeysuckle and injections of mistletoe. They were as lonely as two peas alone in an enormous pod. They hated the idea of Gothic Cottage standing empty. Buck was not good at leaving things tidy. The trail of muddle he left behind him in certain rooms was deeply impregnated with him. One day Hamsyn found his wife brooding there, while the children slept in their pram.

'Do you like it that much?' he asked.

Judy had always liked the big house best, but something in her resisted saying so.

'Shall we move down here?' he asked her. 'Shall I do it up for you?'

'We'd have to do it up,' she said. 'It reminds me so much of Buck as it is now. Do you think we treated him very badly?'

'Oh no,' said Hamsyn. 'I still love him, don't you? Anyway, why don't we live in both houses?'

For the time being, that seemed to be a solution. But although Buck as a presence had become an ache to Judy, as an absence he settled into being a deeper affliction to her.

New Yorker

Dear Hamsyn,

Thank you for sending on all my things. Air Freight must have cost you a bomb; it was very generous. Could you thank Judy for her letter to me and say I will answer soon, but at present I am too dazed by the pace of New York to write a proper letter, which hers demands.

Glad to hear you are moving into Gothic Cottage, which as you know is my favourite place on earth. I will haunt you more conveniently there, and hope you will keep me a spare room. My things still being there did represent a kind of toehold, but of course you are quite right to use it.

How are Tick-Tock and Jammy? I must say I wish they were mine, but they have Haddalot eyes.

Best,

Buck

P.S. Who should I run into on Fifth Avenue of all places but Dizzy? We whooped and swooped. She sends love. I said I was your lodger, which she hadn't heard, and that you'd married, which she had. She is training to be a child psychiatrist. I would find her too tough if I were a child, but I expect Tick-Tock and Jammy would stand up to her. She wanted to know all about you; I didn't quite know what to say. Please instruct. Don't forget to tell Judy I'll write soon as I can. Better not tell her about Dizzy.

Buck

Of course Hamsyn did show Judy this letter. He was too fascinated by the thought of Buck and Dizzy taking up their old affair to be able to keep it to himself. Anyway, he thought Judy ought to know. He was right about that, because the news, which she was certain must be true, freed her from a load of guilt. At the same time she eyed Hamsyn speculatively. Was his guiding passion a long- ing for some kind of incest? She decided that she did not care much. If Tocsin and Jasmine wanted to commit incest, she thought, she would not mind in the least. They crooned and crowed together, as happy as the day was long.

No more news came from America. Gothic Cottage was painted gold and white inside and whitewashed outside. Judy painted the furniture gold and white and Hamsyn bought her gold and white embroidered cur- tains, double-lined against the light. The Georgian Society complained to the Ministry of the Environment, but by then it was too late. The goats in the park bred like rabbits, the plovers and the seagulls did not cease to lay. Hamsyn developed a taste for jackdaws' eggs, which he collected for himself with a ladder and a soup ladle, and brought them home in Tick-Tock's pram. The twins now had a pram each: Judy thought they would never be so happy again. She may have been right. The little family began to forget about Buck. Hamsyn began to feel he was grown up at last. They all still felt a warm affection for each other all the same. They often went over the ground of their memories, hoping to understand one another. Dizzy and Buck were lost to the other two; they were also lost to one another, but they were still held together by a secret magnetism. Buck could never really disentangle himself. Dizzy was never really willing to let him go. They drifted from scrape into scrape, all over again.

It is often harder to tell when an affair is over than when it begins, and harder still with a whole cobweb of various affairs, a mating group who recognize one another by mysterious signals not consciously known. Buck had found himself a new world and discovered it was only a family, he had been sucked into the family and held more tightly by it the more he was spat out. When he looked back, everything that had happened to him felt inevitable from beginning to end. He knew in his bones that the Haddalots had not finished with him, nor had he with them. There were going to be no clean edges. He wondered if what he had discovered was really the love of his life or just some disgraceful weakness in himself, something he was born with or something to do with Weston-super-Mare. However that might be, he saw these last few years as the material or the governing background of his future poetry. If only he could write it, but for more than one reason he could not. Kissing and telling demands a coldness or a nastiness he had not yet achieved, though he was working on it. He was going to achieve it in the end. And does the road wind uphill all the way? Yes, to the very end. And does the journey take the livelong day? From morn to night, my friend. That, he told himself, was his epitaph as a social climber. He suspected it was also the story of his life to come. He intended to lead that life in America. In England, the vicars were grinning like alligators behind every hedge.